THE HUNT

FOR

FOREST CROWN

By

Michael Westborn

EDITED BY

KRYSTINE Mc CORMICK

OVERTON NEVADA

D1277328

CHAPTER

1

The Colorado summer was slowly fading and giving way to the slightly cooler fall. The leaves on the trees had not yet begun to change, that was still several weeks away. The days were still hot, but not the kinf of sweltering heat that meant summer in southeast Colorado. The three-year-old stallion trotted proudly around the corral and whinnied as Jake picked himself up out of the soft dirt. That's when he saw a lone rider appear from around the house and head directly for the corral. Jake could see he wasn't armed and by the way he sat his mount that he was no more than a kid. He picked up his hat and was slapping the dust and dirt off his legs and shirt when the boy Jake now recognized as Cliff, the stable boy from town reined in.

"You been spending a lot of time in the dirt Jake?" Cliff asked, chuckling. Jake smiled while he slapped more dirt off his legs.

"What brings you this far from town, Cliff?" Jake asked. Jake noticed Cliff's horse was breathing hard and was shiny from sweat it showed the horse had been ridden hard. "This morning two men rode into the stable. While they were unsaddling, they started asking questions about the red-headed Marshall and the fella that rode with him. I told them I didn't know ya. Then they started asking at the hotel about you. Mary played dumb, she said she just moved to town and didn't know you. She figured you might want to know, so here I'm."

Jake pulled his holster off the corral post and strapped it around his waist. Hearing this made him uneasy. People who asked questions always stood out like a skunk at a Sunday picnic.

"You got any idea where they're from?" Jake asked. "They didn't say Jake, but I can tell you this: they're both gun hands. I didn't like 'em when I seen em." "How are they mounted?" Jake asked. "The tall guy rides a long-legged, lean buckskin; the other fella rides a black. Both horses wear the Crown brand." Hearing this, Jake's head snapped around and memories flooded his mind as he looked at the boy.

Jake knew all too well why they were here. He remembered when two of Crown's henchmen beat him nearly to death and stole his horse, Saber leaving him for dead on an alkali flat. Battered and bloody beyond recognition, Pat several weeks to bring him back from the shadows of death.

After more than six weeks of healing, Jake could finally sit a horse and wield a gun. He remembered going to the Crown ranch to reclaim his horse and exact revenge on the man that stole it. He also recalled riding away with saber and leaving the ranch house in flames as Crown promised revenge. The boy could tell, Jake had heard something that grabbed his attention, Jake just nodded and looked off towards Pat's place.

"That animal reminds me of his daddy, don't he Jake? I'll finish him off for you guaranteed. For two dollars, you'll be able to sit that wild beast when I'm through." Jake nodded in agreement and opened the gate for the lanky kid. Cliff was nearly six feet tall his hair was a little long and he wore a knife on his side, which was common. Maybe he would tip the beam at one-hundred fifty pounds fully dressed, but no more.

Jake had heard the boy could ride, so he moved over and pushed the young horse against the tall corral posts, grabbing him by the reins. Just as the boy approached, the wheezing horse reached out and bit Jake on the left arm. Jake quickly pulled his arm away from the horse's grip. In a lightning-fast move, he doubled up his right fist and planted a solid punch directly on the jaw of the unruly young horse.

"Hold him Jake' till I tell ya, then you let him go." Jake held both reins just below the bitt while Cliff climbed into the saddle of the fidgeting young horse. Once there, he took the reins and yanked them tight, pulling the horses chin down. He wrapped the reins around the pommel and tucked the finger on his right hand around the base of the horn, then he turned slightly in the saddle and tucked the fingers of his left hand under the back of the saddle and told Jake to let him go.

The young, partially broke stallion instantly jumped two feet into the air and tried with everything he had to throw the young kid to the ground just as he had done with Jake so many times that morning. Jake backed away knowing Cliff would soon pile up in the dirt just as he had done.

As he watched the kid, he quickly learned this young lad had done this before. Jake had never seen anyone grab a saddle like that: it was plain the boy had a death grip on the saddle and had no intention of tasting dirt this day.

While he watched the stable boy, the words Crown Ranch wouldn't leave his mind. Still, he couldn't take his eyes off the boy who looked as though he was tied to the saddle. He knew there was trouble and he knew why. Pat had been gone several days and was due back tomorrow.

After about half an hour the angry young stallion began to slow down. Then. Unexpectedly, he stopped bucking and Cliff loosened the reins from the horn and rode the tired young horse in nonstop circles around the large corral.

"Open the gate Jake," the boy called. Jake moved over and swung the gate wide open and watched the wild-eyed stallion bolt through, nearly running him over. Quickly, Jake stepped aside and watched Cliff ride off into the grassy fields of the Rising Sun Ranch. Jake thought that was the best two bucks he'd ever spent.

He couldn't get out of his mind the message

the young boy had brought him. To Jake it was more than a message, it was a warning. Jake stood and stared at the stallion with the boy atop fading into the distance at a dead run. He didn't have long to wait before the horse and boy reappeared, coming hard and fast.

Jake watched the stampeding horse take a sharp fast right. He bucked a little, but he couldn't lose the kid. As he got closer, Jake watched the boy set his spurs and move the stallion to an even faster pace, then he reined the sweaty animal to the left and again put iron to the horse's flank incredibly the horse moved even faster.

That young horse is as fast as Saber, Jake thought. Then he saw the horse come to a skidding stop, the boy then nudging him to a gentle walk back to the corral. Once again Jake reached over and pulled the gate open and stood aside as the beautiful black and gray pranced proudly through the gate.

Dropping the reins to the ground, Cliff smoothly slid out of the saddle. Both cliff and the horse were tired, sweaty, and breathing hard it was plain they were near spent.

"He's a strong horse Jake, you unsaddle him

and he'll like you for that. He ain't too fond of me now. Until you and him come to an understanding, don't try to tie him off with the reins. He's still some wild, what he needs now is a friend. You might want to take him for a ride. That's one hell of a horse Jake, he's just like his daddy," Cliff said. Quickly, he stretched his hand out for his two dollars. Jake smiled and dropped a five-dollar gold piece in the kid's hand. The boy looked up at Jake as if to say, *I don't have change.*

"I need you to do something for me Cliff, I need you to ride out back beyond the pond and send Joe and Web up to the house now. Then, most important, Pat took two prisoners up to that pen in Canon. He's due back on tomorrows train. I want you waiting there with his horse saddled when he steps off the train.

You tell him I need him to hot foot it out here. You keep this under your hat and you've earned the three extra. Don't miss the train."

The young boy smiled and climbed back on his sweaty horse then headed for the pond. Jake could tell Cliff rode the horse hare getting here. Jake watched the boy mount up and ride out but what he really had in mind was the warning the boy brought him. Jake and Pat were close to the people in Las Animas, but he didn't know if anyone would answer the questions that were being asked around town.

Jake turned and saw Jodie hoeing weeds in the garden next to the house. Her coal black hair was mostly covered with a white bonnet but it couldn't cover the black curls that lay on her back. He already had a pretty good idea of what was to be but right now, he had to tell her why there would be house guests this night.

Sharon was the only neighbor for miles, over time she and Jodie had become close friends. They both lived in fear every time their husbands rode out together. They only had each other to talk to and share their thoughts and worries with. Both were afraid their husband's way of life would someday catch up with them. Sharon didn't blame Jake and Jodi didn't blame Pat. They both had come to realize the wild untamed in both their men was a part of their soul. Their greatest uncontrollable fear was that one day one of them would bring the other home tied over a saddle.

They both knew these two men had protected and kept each other alive on numerous occasions. When Sharon met Pat, she had just been widowed and Pat was there to comfort and protect her and her two young kids. She had a small ranch and half a hundred head of stock in the pasture she needed to sell and that's where Pat came in. She had two small children and they were her first and main concern. But over time she grew to rely on Pat's protection and kindness. She knew her son would need a father and she saw in Pat a willingness to care for the young ones, but she never considered the way he lived and she didn't see the wildness in him at first.

That all changed with time. Now, she knew he had a streak of wildness in him that was always hidden but just below the surface.

When Jodie saw Jake coming, she straighten up and untied the strings on her bonnet. "Let's have a cup of coffee," he said. "That sounds good Jake," she replied. Then she turned and walked at his side to the house. She knew he had something on his mind and was about to share it.

While she stood by the sink pumping water into the gray porcelain coffee pot, Jake threw some small wood into the stove in the kitchen. He then dropped down into the nearest chair at the table and stared out the window.

"What's on your mind Jake,? you seem a little troubled," She said. Jake just stared forward watching Joe and Web who were several hundred yards off coming to the house. Before the coffee was ready, Jake stepped out the back door letting the screen slam shut. The loud crack of the door made Jodie jump a little. The men hadn't had time to dismount when Jake appeared.

"Don't climb down, go over to the bunk house and get your rifles. Then go to Pat's, hitch up his wagon and bring Sharon and the kids to the house. If you see someone you don't recognize don't let them get within three-hundred yards of ya. You come back through the east gate and through the fields, keep on your toes," Jake said.

Jodie stood behind the screen and listened and watched. Hearing what she did, gave her cold chills, she then knew there was trouble with Pat and it had to be bad. She had learned over time, when there was trouble for Jake or Pat then there was trouble for both. They were closer than brothers.

The two hands reined around and set their

spurs. Jake turned and saw Jodie standing at the door. "Well, I guess you pretty much figured we're having house guests tonight."

"Me and the boy will sleep in the bunk house with the hands, you and Sharon will have the house with the girl tonight." Jake turned and walked to the rifle cabinet that hung on the wall near the corner in the living-room. There were at least a half dozen rifles and a short, barreled shotgun. He didn't need to load the rifles, every gun in the house was kept loaded. Jake took down the double barrel shotgun from the rack, cracked it open to check the fill, then took it into the bedroom. He wouldn't be in the house this night; this gun was for Jodie.

"You figuring on telling me what's up, Jake?" Jake walked over to the stove and poured two cups of hot coffee then walked back to the divan and handed Jodie the steaming cup. Then he dropped down in a wing back chair across the room.

"Seems as though there's a couple men in town asking about me and Pat. I know from what they're riding, where they came from, and I know why they're here. They're here for no good. As I look back on it now, I realize now I shouldn't have left that old bastard alive," Jake said.

Jodie never sipped the too hot coffee, she just looked at the floor. "I won't leave you or Sharon alone, there will always be the two hands here." "Jake, Web is just a boy, what do you expect him to do?" Jodie said. "Don't underestimate him, I seen him when the heat is on, I saw him shoot a horse thief right in the face. He's got a tub of guts and he can shoot. As far as Joe, don't worry about him, he's been watching my back since I met him. He's the last of my worries."

Jodie got up and walked into the bedroom and returned with two wool blankets and a pair of striped pillows. A small pistol was laying on top of the bedding. Jodie handed Jake the bedding then took the small pistol, walked to the gun cabinet, and dropped it in a drawer.

"I'll go make up the beds in the bunk house Jake," Jodie said. Jake replied, "Pat will be here tomorrow, we'll ride into town and clean up this mess and I hope it'll all be over."

In a little less than two hours the wagon rolled up to the back door. Web had his horse tied to the back of the wagon and sat next to Sharon with a Winchester lying across his lap. Sharon was wearing a wide brimmed straw summer hat; the two kids rode in the back sitting on a sack of grain. Joe had his rifle propped on his leg with the barrel skyward riding some twenty yards behind.

Jodie stepped out on the back porch to greet her friend just in time to hear the kid's scream "Hi Jodie." Before she could say anything, Sharon pressed and said, "what is going on?" While Sharon climbed down from the wagon Jodie said, "I'll tell you what I know, come on in out of the heat."

Just then Jake walked up and grabbed a canvas bag out of the back of the wagon, then glanced over at Joe. "Didn't see a soul, Jake." "Take them horses to the barn and unsaddle 'em, then we'll talk," Jake said. He walked into the house and dropped his hat on the table. Jodie walked over, picked it up, and hung it on a peg in the wall.

Sharon stood silent and waited for an explanation as to why she and her kids were taken out of their home without a word. Then she broke her silence. "I wanna know what's going on, Jake

Cleary," she said in a loud defiant tone.

"There's some fellas in town asking questions about Jake and Pat. Jake isn't quite sure of what they want, so to be on the safe side, he wanted you here. He said Pat will come here first when he gets to town but until then, he would feel better knowing you're not alone," Jodie said.

Sharon smiled and nodded politely. "Joe and Web will go over and feed and water this evening," Jake said. "Josh and Jake will be sleeping in the bunk house tonight, you me and Emily will have the house to ourselves," Jodie said. "Josh will like sleeping in the bunk house with the men," Sharon commented.

It was late afternoon when the two fully armed hands, mounted up and headed for the Two Rivers ranch. Pat had several head of horses and some chickens that needed fed. When they got there Joe moved the horses from the big corral to the corral that was attached to the barn. Web grabbed a pitchfork and started stacking hay inside the barn while Joe started carrying water to the though. Once the horses were inside, Joe pushed the barn door shut, keeping the horses out of sight. Web scattered a couple handfuls of scratch on the ground for the chickens.

The sun was low in the west and the two cut a fast trail for the Rising sun as Jake had told them "Don't let the sun set on ya before you get here." When they got to the barn Jake was headed into the bunk house with two boxes of bullets in one hand and a Winchester in the other.

The two dropped the saddles on the horses and were rubbing them down when they heard Jodie calling for dinner. Quickly, Joe and Web splashed some water over their faces, and dried on their sleeves, then set a trail for the house. Ever since Jodie arrived at the ranch the food had greatly improved and kept the men happy.

After a quick dinner, Jake and the two hands stepped out on the back porch with a near empty bottle of whisky and three small glasses. "Once the sun is down Web, I want you to get a Winchester and take your bed roll out under that cottonwood." Jake pointed to the giant tree where his family rested. Make your bed up there. You sleep light, if you see or hear anyone you let us know." Then Jake glanced down at the rifle. Web knew exactly what he meant.

They sat a while and when the curtain of

night covered everything Joe and Web headed for the bunk house. Jake walked back into the house and pulled down all the shades on all the windows and twisted the locks. Jodie pushed two padded chairs together making a small bed for the young girl.

CHAPTER

2

Jake walked in and looked around. He remembered spending a winter in the cold barn with the horses and a couple goats until the bunk house was ready. You couldn't put a stove in the barn, that was asking for trouble. That was several years back and he kinda liked that bunk house. Pat, Joe and him scrambled to get it done so they could sleep somewhere besides a stinking barn. No matter how clean the barn was they had that smell you never grew accustomed to.

Joe and Web had all the windows propped open with sticks to pull in the cool night air. An oil lamp sat on the cold stove; they had no need to light the stove: it was too hot this time of the year.

Jake leaned his Winchester against the wall

next to his bed, unbuckled his holster and hung it on a peg. He then dropped down on an empty cot and there he pulled off his boots. He didn't bother to drop his trousers, he just laid back and rested his pistol on his chest as always. Joe walked over and smothered the flame on the lamp and Jake dozed off in a very light sleep.

What awoke Jake was the silent gray light moving across the floor. It was just about sunup when he started pulling on his boots. He sat on the small bunk and looked around. He couldn't remember the last time he hadn't see the sunrise. It had been that way all his life and he liked it that way. He looked over at Joe and knew why he could sleep that solid, but a man who lived like Jake could never do that.

Jake stepped to the door to see the morning sunrise and feel the cool air. Joe sat up and rubbed his eyes when he heard the door squeak. Jake looked over to the cottonwoods to see Web leaned back asleep against the tree with a rifle in his arms.

He had come to know and trust Web more as the kid aged. He had gained a mountain of respect for the boy when he had seen him beat the hell out of a giant of a man with an ax handle who bullied him. Now, standing in the door of the bunk house, he waited for Pat to ride up. The two would then ride into town and deal with the problem from the Crown Ranch. Hearing the name Crown ranch brought back memories of a very black time in his life :when he actually looked forward to killing a man he didn't even know.

He knew the train from Canon City would be in sometime between eight and nine if on schedule. Web awoke and saw Jake, so he got to his feet, then grabbed his blanket and started for the bunk house. Joe pulled on his boots and grabbed his hat, then strapped his Colt around his waist. "After you get something in your belly, you and Web go over and take care of Pat's stock, then get back here and keep an eye out," Jake said. Then he picked up his rifle and headed for the house.

"I could smell the coffee before I got here," he said as the screen door slammed. Jodie, still wrapped in a flowered chenille robe, pulled several cups down off their hooks and begin pouring the steaming coffee. Just then, Joe and Web came to the back door. both men were carrying rifles. Usually, they would announce then set themselves down, but today was different and they knew it.

Jodie handed each a steaming cup and the three walked over and sat on the edge of the porch. "You get done at Pat's high tail it back here. Stay near the house till I say different. Don't let any strangers near, if you don't recognize them put a bead on 'em," Jake said.

Jodie and Sharon brought all three a plate loaded with eggs and potatoes to where they sat and handed them the usual fork and knife. Sharon and the kids knew Joe and Web well, they had worked from time to time at the Two Rivers whenever Pat needed help. They both knew it was their job, no, their duty to protect the women when either one or both men were gone.

The boys had finished their morning chow and had gone to Pat's place. Jake had just finished saddling two mounts: the young stallion for himself and the red for Pat: he knew when Pat got there, he would want a fresh horse. Just as he stepped out of the barn, he looked up to see a small cloud of dust coming from where he knew the road was. The road to the ranch set behind a rise that was a little higher than the house making the road impossible to see from the house.

He glanced up at the sun and blocked the glare with his hand, he figured it was a little after ten and that dust would be Pat. Jake knew it had to be Pat but because he couldn't see for sure, he picked up his rifle and watched the trail of dust get closer.

After a couple minutes he saw a single rider crest the hill in front of the house. He knew immediately it was Pat. He then set down the Winchester, he wanted to speak to him away from the ears of the women until he knew exactly what was going on. To jake there was only one way, which was to ride to town and confront the men asking the questions.

Pat rode past the house and reined in, in front of Jake. The two women heard and saw him ride in. "What's so important?" he said as his boots touched dirt. Jake hesitated a second. "Sharon and the kids are up with Jodie; she spent the night. I wanted them close. Pat then knew there was big trouble and he wanted to hear it.

"You remember old man Crown?" Jake asked. Pat answered with a nod. "Well, there's a couple men in town asking about me and you, both their horses are wearing the Crown brand." Pat Just stared at the ground for a minute. "I knew one of us should have shot that old coot when you had him on his knees," Pat said. "I have a fresh horse saddled; I knew you'd want one." Pat just stood and slapped the palm of his gloved hands with his reins as he always did then he nodded in agreement.

Jake took Pat's reins and led the sweaty, white-eyed mare in the barn. While Jake unsaddled the tired horse, Pat turned and headed for the house. He needed to unstiffen a little and he wanted to talk to Sharon. He knew it was the boy's birthday and he wanted to talk to him before he rode out.

Jake pulled Pat's Winchester out of his scabbard and slid it into the one on the red. He heard the screen door slam as he was putting an extra lead rope on the young stallion. He had been warned not to trust the young, half wild horse, and Jake was going to heed the warning.

By the time Jake got to the house, Pat was standing on the back porch. He had Sharon's hand clutched in his while the young girl held on to her dress and the boy stood off to the side and watched. Josh remembered his dad, he remembered him leaving for town and never seeing him again, then one day the big red-headed man was there trying to take his place and he was confused.

Pat leaned over gently kissing the pretty Sharon and said, "I'll be home for dinner. He looked at the boy and said "I might be bringing you home a present, so you look out for your mom." Josh smiled and said, "Ok Pat." Jodie smiled at Jake and said, "You be careful Jake, if you have to shoot, shoot first." He could tell by the look in her eyes and the tone of her voice her comment to shoot first wasn't a half-hearted comment, she meant it. Jake nodded and climbed into the saddle of the half wild horse that had yet to be named.

When Pat climbed into the saddle, they slowly walked their horses down the ruts and out of sight. Once over the rise, they moved to a faster pace and headed for the peaceful town of Las Animas where they knew two men were hunting them.

They didn't have to be told, they knew why

the two strangers they hadn't seen yet were in town. They knew Forest Crown was a rich man who was accustomed to having things his way and having men bow to his wishes. They knew he built his empire and held it together with hired gunmen.

Many times, the two rode together into trouble and one way or another they always rode back. When the town came into sight, Jake reined left with Pat close at his side they rode to the back of the livery stable. Before they dismounted, Jake checked the fill of his Colt. "I'll go in first Pat, they're looking for the red- headed marshall." Jake took the reins of the fidgety horse and the lead rope and walked around front and through the open doors of the stable. After a moment Pat led the red through the doors to see Jake talking to Cliff the stable boy.

"Them two fellas from the Crown ranch still here, Cliff?" Jake asked. "Yeah, those their horses right there Jake, that tall one is a good horse," he answered as he pointed to the two back stalls. Pat walked over to the stall and looked at the horses then looked at Jake and nodded. "That tall one is a good-looking horse," Pat said.

"Marshall, I got these two pegged as back shooters, so you keep 'em in front of ya," Cliff said, then he handed Jake a bullet. "I seen one of them drop this." What he handed Jake was a rim fire forty-one caliber bullet. That particular bullet was used in a two-barrel Remington derringer. It was mainly used by gamblers and saloon girls. It was a low yield round usually used for backup; at very close range it was as deadly as any bullet. Jake bounced the small cartridge in his hand then he handed it to Pat. "You know where they're at now Cliff," Pat asked. "I can't say Pat probably at one of the saloons," he replied.

It was midafternoon and the sun was beating down as always. The two men left the stable and headed for Front Street. In Las Animas businesses and stores set on both sides of the street as in all western towns. There were shops and stores, offices, a mercantile, saloons, a barber shop, and a small tin shop. Las Animas even had its own dentist and a doctor. It normally was a peaceful little town.

Cautiously, the two stepped from between two buildings and peered up and down both sides of the dry dusty street looking for strangers. "Pat,

I'm going to check at the hotel and see what Mary has to say." "I'm going to stop by the sheriff's office and see what he knows," Pat said.

Jake turned left as he crossed the street. A slight breeze came up and lifted the dust and pushed a small tumbleweed down the dusty road. Jake noticed very few people were out and about, he thought they were probably trying to stay out of the heat. As he walked, the only sound was the heels of his boots on the boardwalk and the ringing of his spurs.

The pleasant smell of baking bread coming from the café filled his nose, reminding him of his mother. This pleased him. As he passed the café, he quickly glanced through the window as he walked past. The café sat next to a dress shop, then there was a narrow space between that building and the hotel. Cautiously, he looked down the narrow alley as he passed, then he walked into the only hotel in town. As usual, Mary Allard with her honey-colored hair stood behind the tall counter. She smiled when Jake walked in.

Mary and Jake grew up together. She had been in love with him since she could remember. She always had an idea she and Jake would someday marry, but Jodie came into the picture and put an end to Mary's hopes for the future. Jake respectfully took off his hat. "Hello Mary, you look well as always," Jake said. Mary blushed and smiled, "I know why you're here; I can see Cliff told you about the strangers," she said. "What they ask you?" Jake asked. "Mostly about Pat, they didn't know your name so I lied to 'em, they're trouble Jake.

The shortest one wears a long black mustache and chin whiskers, don't turn your back on him," she said. "You see them around this morning?" Jake asked. "I think you just walked by the tall one, I think he's in the café. I saw him cross the street a little while ago," she grinned, unless he went in the dress shop." Jake turned and glanced out the window.

Pat walked in the lawman's office and dropped down in a chair across from the town sheriff. Willard had been the sheriff for several years and Pat knew him well. "Willard, you seen them strangers in town been asking questions?" "Yeah, I seen 'em, they haven't done anything so I let them be but I don't like 'em. They got trouble writ all over 'em. I sent a wire to Denver and Santa

Fe but." I got nothing back on 'em. Pat got up and headed up the street for the hotel.

Jake cautiously left the hotel and stepped off the boardwalk into the narrow alley next to the dress shop and waited. After a couple minutes he saw Pat coming up the boardwalk. This he didn't like, Pat was armed with his rifle as usual, putting him at a big disadvantage: he could never bring the rifle into position before a professional gunman could draw and fire.

Silently, Jake watched. Just as Pat stepped into the hotel the tall stranger walked out of the café and stepped into the open.

The gun fighter was well over six-feet tall, well dressed, and slender. He wore garters holding down the sleeves on his blue shirt just below his elbows. He packed a Remington with black grips slung low and tied down. There was no mistaking this guy, he was a professional gunfighter and hired killer. He had a boney well shaved face with high cheek bones and a sharp pointed nose that was a slightly too long for his face. He was dark skinned with dark eyes and looked like he was, or could be, part Indian. He was what was what one might call rat faced. His pants were tucked in the tops of his well-shined boots. Where he stood his large, brimmed hat shaded his squinty eyes from the bright sun.

Jake flipped the tie on his Colt. Little more than twenty-five separated the two. Before the tall man could speak, Jake stepped to his right putting him at the stranger's right side.

"I hear tell you been asking questions about me, you got something you want to say?" Jake asked in a loud commanding voice.

Hearing the voice on his right, the tall man turned and stepped forward slightly to see Jake slowly circling putting the sun at his back . Once the gunman saw Jake, he flipped the tie on his pistol as he turned slightly too face him.

"You think that old man forgot? Well, we're here to tell you, he didn't." The few people that were on the boardwalk that saw Jake confront the gunman, stepped through the nearest door, and watched through the windows. They knew there was going to be gun play and they knew the stranger was about to die.

There was maybe twenty feet separating them when Jake's hand flashed for his gun. Before the tall stranger could drop his hand for his iron,

Jake had cleared leather and started to fanned his Colt. The first slug caught him directly in the stomach, pushing him backwards while Jake kept moving forward cocking and firing.

As the gunman struggled to get his footing, Jake re cocked and fired again and again. By the time, the second bullet buried itself in the tall gunman, he had his pistol out of the holster. As the third bullet hit him, his pistol roared and the slug took out the window of the dress shop. When the third bullet came out his back he staggered and fell face down in the dusty street. Instantly, a pool of blood formed around him and begin to soak into the dry dirt.

Hearing the shots Pat with his rifle at its ready, came out of the hotel and walked up to Jake who was standing over the dead man. "I wasn't fooling with this guy Pat, I wasn't gonna let him touch that pistol. I've had enough holes in me," Jake said. "Jodie was right, if you gotta shoot, shoot first," Pat said. Jake smiled and agreed with a nod.

By now people started to gather to see the man that went up against Jake Cleary. Pat bent over and picked up the pistol that filled the gunman's hand and handed it to Jake. "I guess this is yours now," Pat said. Jake handed it back to Pat and he tucked it behind his belt.

Pat grabbed the gunman by the arm and rolled him over to see his face and turn out his pockets in hopes of finding something so he could put a name to him. When he turned out the first pocket, he was surprised when a half dozen double eagled and two five-dollar gold pieces fell to the ground. In the other pocket he had only a common single- bladed Barlow knife.

The patrons in the saloon gathered in the road to see what had just happened, several were still holding their beer mugs as they gawked and talked.

Jake looked around, Pat knew who he was looking for, then he saw the apron clad bartender who stood in the crowd. He never had to say a word. The man with the apron, like most everyone in town, grew up with Jake and liked him. "Jake, if you're looking for the fella that rides with him, he's over in the saloon. He's been in there since I opened up, sipping coffee. He's at the front end of the bar.

Jake and Pat looked at each other, then

Jake flipped the gate on his Colt and shucked the empty brass into the dirt. He pulled three fresh shells from his belt and slid them into the cylinder. He had more business to take care of after all, it was him who burnt Crowns house not Pat and the way he figured it, this man was here for him. Jake turned and started walking away. Just then two small boys rushed in and scrambled through the dirt to pick up the empty shell that lay beside the body of the gunman whose name was yet to be known.

As he walked the crowd separated to let him pass. With Pat at his side, he made his way down the boardwalk with his pistol in hand. Pat carried his Winchester, but now he had a Remington six-shooter stuffed in his belt.

The 1875 Remington was comparable to the Colt, it just didn't have the same reputation and they weren't as available in the west. The crowd watched and stood back as the two made their way to the saloon.

Hearing the shots, the traveler knew either way someone would come through those doors. To gain an edge, he reached down and racked the hammer on his Colt and left it to rest in his holster but Jake would not know this.

Mary Allerd stood across the street and watched with fear as Jake stepped into the saloon to face a traveling gunman he had not yet seen. Pat held back and let Jake step through the door first. When the traveling gunman saw Jake, it was too late. Jake had his iron in his hand hanging loosely at his side. Seeing the big cowboy, the traveler now knew who he hunted.

He wasn't what one would call a big man, he was under six- feet tall with broad shoulders and thick arms. He wore a well-used, sweat stained, brown hat. He wasn't a flashy dresser, no garters, shiny boots, or showy vest, but he did wear a large turquoise ring on his left hand. His shiny, black holster was filled with a stag handled Colt that looked well cared for like it was his prize possession. He wore the black- facial hair just as Mary had described.

When Jake walked in the gunman had a coffee cup in his right hand, which he quickly set down. Then he noticed Jake's hand hanging at his side was full of iron.

Only seconds had passed and the traveling gunfighter knew he had to move quickly or the big cowboy would take him. In the blink of an eye, he swept the cup off the bar with his left hand in Jake's direction to distract him as he went for his Colt at the same time.

When Jake saw the gunman's, left hand move for the cup, he dove to the left and raised his pistol just before he hit the floor hard. Then, with the roar of the gunman's Colt, Jake felt a sharp stinging pain run across the top of his left forearm just above his elbow.   Jake, whose gun was in play the instant he saw the gunman's hand move dropped the hammer and the traveling gun fighter folded in the middle and drop his pistol to the floor.

Jake instantly cocked his pistol and clambered to his feet. With a slight stinging in his left arm and a trickle of blood running down his sleeve, he walked up to the man who was spitting blood and turned him over. Pat quickly walked to his side.

"Where is Crown?" Jake demanded. The gunman chocked a little before he spoke. "He'll be along and he don't go nowhere alone." Slowly, his lips formed a slight smile and his eyes glazed over as he stopped breathing.

Jake reached over and picked up his cocked pistol and realized the young gunman had got off a shot and re cocked before Jake fired. With this thought, Jake relaxed the hammer on the gunman's pistol. Pat looked at Jake, they were both thinking the same thing. *This isn't over, it's just the start.*

CHAPTER

3

Pat knelt down and turned out the dead gunman's front pocket. After what he had just seen in the street he wasn't at all surprised when three double eagles and two eagles fell to the floor. It wasn't common for a man to be carrying one hundred-twenty dollars in gold but, he knew hired gunmen were well paid and this time he knew who paid them.

When he dumped the other pocket, he found only a sterling silver match safe, "Let's check his room, maybe we can find out who this guy is and where he's from," Pat said. From there they walked across the street to the hotel. When they walked in, Jake saw Mary and he could tell she was what one would call kind of upset. They didn't have to ask, she just handed Jake two room keys. Jake nodded to her politely and handed one of the keys to Pat then the two headed up the stairs.

The room was small, as were most all hotel rooms in Las Animas. Jake looked around and saw a pair of saddle bags piled up on the floor next to a small dresser. A white porcelain bowl with a matching pitcher sat in front of a mirror that hung on the wall above the dresser. Jake took a single step and dumped the saddle bags on the small, unmade bed. What hit the blanket was a fixed blade knife and a small half empty bottle of whiskey. What landed on top was a well-worn, once white shirt.

Jake looked in the bottom of one side of the bag, jammed in the corner was a piece of brown, heavy paper that looked as though it had been folded and refolded countless times. When Jake unfolded the paper, he saw a bill of sale for a brown horse with three stockings to a William Pate.

This was a name Jake and half the people in Colorado had heard. William Pate was a well-known gunfighter out of New Mexico, he had a reputation that stemmed from more than two dozen gun fights in New Mexico, Arizona, and

Nevada. According to his reputation all the encounters were fair and open deadly contests of speed.

Pat opened the door and looked from side to side, a pair of saddle bag hung over the metal foot board. Just as Jake did, he dumped the bags across the bed. What he found was what he himself might carry in his bags. A bone handled knife and what looked to be a brass watch, but Pat recognized it as a military compass. A small tin box filled with sulfur matches along with a fairly new shirt. A small leather fold up binder looked like a large, men's wallet. When he untied the leather, he found a letter giving Marvin Allen ownership of one-hundred sixty acres near Flagstaff, Arizona. *Even a guy like this had or wanted a different way of life,* Pat thought.

As a US Marshall, Pat had heard the name Marvin Allen in his travels. He was suspected of at least a half dozen killings but nothing could be legally pinned on him. Pat knew he needed killing, the way Pat figured it, time and his lifestyle just caught up with him.

Pat took one of the eagles, gave it to Albert the undertaker and told him to take care of the dead and plant 'em on Boot Hill. "I'll meet you at the livery in a few minutes Jake, I got something I have to do," Pat said. A few minutes later he walked out of the mercantile carrying a Stephens single barrel, twenty-two, crack shot, youth rifle in one hand, while he slid a small box of twenty-two caliber bullets in his shirt pocket. Carrying the small gun, he walked into the livery. "I told the boy I would bring him home a present." Jake looked at him. "It's his birthday." Jake smiled.

Pat reached in his pocket and gave the other eagle to Cliff and told him to take care of their horses. Cliff asked Jake what would be done with those two horses. "We'll have to wait and see, chances are the owner might be coming for them, maybe he will maybe he won't. If he doesn't, you can have your pick," Jake said. Pat looked at Cliff and said with a grin. "Keep the tall one it's the better of the two."

The boy smiled and they mounted up, then Pat pulled a bottle of whiskey out of his bags, took a big swallow, and passed the bottle off to Jake. After a mouthful, Jake handed the bottle to Cliff and they set their spurs heading back to where their nervous wives waited.

The ride back to the ranch was quiet, it was obvious both men were thinking about old man Crown and the problems that were yet to come. Jake reined in at the rise and looked down at his ranch. Pat stopped at his side. "I think we have a few days until Crown finds out his money got his men killed," Jake said.

Hearing the word money, Pat reached back in his saddle bag and pulled out the leather binder and handed it to Jake. "Here are those coins our gunman had, I guess they're yours now," Pat said. Jake opened the leather pouch and handed Pat five of the twenty-dollar gold coins. Pat stood in the stirrups and slid the gold into his front pocket.

"You know our weak spot, don't you Pat?" "Yeah, I know, but I got to think on it a while," Pat said. Gently, Jake touched the young horse with his spurs and the two followed the ruts to the front of the barn with Pat carrying the small rifle across his saddle bows. Just as their boots touched the ground, they heard the screen door slap shut. Pat turned to see the two women standing on the porch and Josh running towards them. "Pat, you said you'd be home for dinner. "Did you bring me a present, Pat?" The excited boy asked. Pat reached out and handed the boy the rifle. Josh took the gun and went running back to the porch with the rifle in hand. "Look what Pat brought me, mom, it's a beauty," he said. Sharon smiled and looked at Jodie. "It's his birthday." Jodie smiled.

Just then, Joe and Web walked up to the two tired men. "We'll take the horses Jake, you go on in and get a bite to eat," Joe said. "Web, will you saddle my horse and hitch up the wagon?" After I get a bite to eat, we'll be heading home." Pat said. Web answered with nod.

Jake looked at Jodie and put his arm around her. As she laid her head on his chest, he said, "I'll tell you everything later, now I would like to get something to eat." "Ok Jake, Joe and Web already had dinner," Jodie said. Jake, Pat and the two young ones calmly sat down while the two ladies cut the roast and filled plates. While they were eating, they heard the clatter of the wagon pulling up to the back porch.

It was dark when the wagon rolled up to the gate that closed off Pat's place. Josh jumped off the wagon with his new rifle in hand and swung the gate wide. Pat slapped the back of the horses with the reins and steered the team to the front of the barn. After he helped Sharon down, she walked to the porch and lit an oil lamp to see her way into the house. Pat reached in just beyond the barn door and took a lantern to the wagon. He needed the light to unhitch the team. The morning of the next day found Jake and Pat both saddling horses. The nights rest wasn't much, they both had too much on their minds to get a good night's sleep. They'd both faced problems like this before but this time they had women and kids that figured into the problem, and that changed everything.

Jake had an idea. They were a mile apart and it was mid-morning when they both swung into the saddle. Jake touched the fidgeting young horse and set a trail across the Rising Sun for Pat's Two Rivers ranch. As it turned out, they met somewhere in between and reined in.

"Pat, I been tossing it around all night and the way I figure it, we'd be better off if we get these women out of here." Pat, listening intently got a slight smile. "We can put 'em on a train and get 'em back to Cripple Creek till this mess is over, Jodie has friends there," Jake said. "Well, that might be fine, Jake but I'd rather have 'em being watched over by Carl, in Durango," Pat added. Jake liked this idea, Durango was farther away and Carl was beholden to them and as good with a gun as anyone he knew.

"I'll go talk to Jodie and let her know the plan. You talk it over with Sharon then we can send a wire to Carl and have him make arrangements for two ladies and the kids," Jake said. Pat agreed with a nod and the two separated and headed back in their own tracks.

Jake walked in the back door of the house to find Jodie rolling up and pounding on a ball of bread dough. The house was now empty, all she wore was a long apron with an open back. To Jake this was an invitation he could not and would not resist. Jodie smiled and wiped the flour off of her hands with a towel. Giggling, she led him into the bedroom where she said three words, "take 'em off." He didn't need to be told, he started unbuttoning his shirt on the way to the bedroom where they made love.   Not quite an hour had passed and Jake was pulling on his shirt when he started telling Jodie of his and Pat's plan. "After what you told me about this fella Crown, I've been expecting something like this," she said as she slipped into her trousers.

Pat rode up to the front of the house and could immediately smell bread being baked in the oven. This helped a little to erase the worry that went with raising a family. In his mind he knew Forest Crown endangered the ones he loved and so he had his mind set, he was going to kill forest Crown one way or another and put an end to the danger. He was surprised when Jake didn't kill him when he had him under his gun back in Wellington. *We would all be a lot better off if he had killed that old man,* he thought.

When Pat rode in he saw the boy by the barn playing with his new rifle. Pat reached in the top of the pantry and took down the box of bullets that came with the gun. "I'm sure he wants to shoot it and I think it's time he learns how," Pat said. Sharon smiled as Pat stepped onto the front porch.

When Josh saw Pat, he went running up with his rifle in hand. "Come on Josh, I'm gonna teach you how to aim and shoot that iron of yours. It was but a few minutes when Sharon started hearing the slight crack of the small rifle.

By the time that box of bullets was gone, the young boy knew how to open, shoulder, aim and shoot the small gun. "Now Josh, if you were rabbit hunting where you would aim to get that rabbit?" Pat asked. "Just like you said aim for the head. "The boy quickly replied. "Someday, and it won't be long, and you'll be hunting rabbits for the table. You remember everything I showed you and you'll do fine," Pat said.

Pat walked back into the house, he was going to explain to Sharon why she must temporarily leave with the kids and go back to Durango. Pat set her down and explained the best he could that not only were her and the kinds in danger but having her here created a weak point for Crown to take advantage of.

Sharon stared into the cup of black coffee and nodded. "Do you think it will be long," she asked. "I don't know but I can't have you and the kids here, not until this is done.," Pat said. "I'm going into town to wire Carl and have him make arrangements for the four of ya," Pat said. "By the way, Josh can hunt rabbits. He may have trouble cleaning them but I'm sure he can shoot 'em," Pat said with a chuckle. Sharon smiled, she wasn't happy about leaving but the safety of the kids was the most important thing to her and Pat.

Pat saddled his white eyed mare and set a trail for town. There were several things he needed before the ladies left, such as ammunition and grub for the house. He also wanted to tell Cliff to keep an eye out for strangers.

When he rode into town, he headed directly for the livery stable. Without dismounting, he bent low and rode right through the front door. Once on the ground he pulled his Winchester free from its scabbard. With things the way they are, Pat's hand would never be without this gun. Cliff stepped through the door carrying a pitchfork and mopping sweat off his forehead. "Howdy Marshall, anything I can do for you today?" he asked. Pat stopped in his tracks and stared at the young kid momentarily.

"What's your deal here Cliff?" Pat asked. "Whatta ya mean Marshall," he replied. Pat came back. "Where do you live, why you working here?" "Mr. Oats pays me ten dollars a month and I sleep here most of the time. It's just me, my mom, three sisters and my brother Clayton. Mom works at the dress shop: she sews, my brother, he hires out to the Miller ranch sometimes," Cliff answered.

"Cliff, I'm looking for a couple hands around my place and you do know horses. I could use someone to take care of my stock. I have some prize cattle out there that's worth a lot of money. I could use a couple good hands, I'll pay you fifteen dollars and your grub," Pat said.

Pat could see a smile begin to form on the boy's face. "You said hands you need someone else?" he asked. "Yeah, if you know someone who's looking, I might be interested," Pat said. "Sure, do Marshall,

Clayton, my older brother, he's been working for the Millers a couple days a week, he wants more time," Cliff answered. Pat nodded his head and said. "Get your stuff together, you be out at my place tomorrow. When I leave here today, I'm taking one of Crown's horses with me, so saddle the other one. In the morning bring the horse out saddled and bring your gear." Pat then turned and headed for the sheriff's office.

When he walked in the office, Willard was leaned back in his chair with his hat pulled down over his face. Pat took off his hat and mopped the sweat from his forehead with his sleeve. He thought Willard was dozing. With the closing of the door the town sheriff slid his hat back uncovering his eyes. "Howdy Pat," he said. Pat plopped down in a chair that sat across the small room. "Albert took care of those two, so that mess is pretty well cleaned up," he said.

"Willard, I'm expecting more visitors and I need you to let me or Jake know as soon as they hit town, especially if you see them riding the Crown brand. I need you to have someone keep an eye out at the train station. You know what to look for," Pat said. Then he went on and told Willard the whole story of why the shootings occurred the day before. The town sheriff sat there and listened to the story of revenge that started more than two years ago

Pat got up and put his hat back on, then started to leave. "One more thing Willard, that stable boy Cliff, you know his brother Clayton?" "I know his whole family, they're good, hard-working people. Clayton can swing a hammer as good as any smith I ever saw and he's only about nineteen years old.

You know him Pat, he won the pistol shooting contest last year at the fourth of July fair." Pat just looked at the sheriff and nodded. With his rifle in hand, he stepped out on the boardwalk and looked up and down the dusty street.

Now he had to send a telegram to Durango and check the schedule, this was most important. When he walked in the telegraph office, he saw Chester pecking away at the key as always. Chester was a little, bald headed, old man, with thick spectacles and a bushy red moustache. He sucked on a cobb pipe endlessly. The first thing you noticed when you walked in was the pipe smoke.

As a US Marshall, Pat had sent uncountable wires to nearly every town in Colorado, New Mexico, Arizona, and Nevada. Now, this time, it was the most important wire he'd ever sent.

"Howdy Pat, you need to send a wire?" Pat nodded and started writing on the yellow pad Chester handed him. "When is the next train to Durango?" he asked. "One left this morning, the next one is day after tomorrow. It pulls out at 9 am sharp, maybe," he said with a slight chuckle.

To- Carl Hockett,

Sheriff, Durango Co.

Carl, sending two women two children soon. Need secure safe place for family. Funds will be delivered on arrival. Women will explain. Your protection required. Wire back with info.
Pat Brennon US Marshal,
Las Animas, Co.

Pat tore the yellow paper off the pad and handed it to the frail old man. He said, "Chester, absolutely no one is to know about this wire. When you get a reply, get it to me or Jake right away." The old clerk, with the pipe hanging out of his mouth, tipped his head down and read the words. Looking over the tops of his glasses he glanced up at Pat. "That'll be two dollars Pat." Pat handed him three silver dollars' and said, "Give the extra to the rider that delivers the answer." With that he turned and left the smoke-filled office.

Pat had one more stop before he returned to the ranch: he promised the boy he would pick him up a box of bullets for his new rifle. While he was at it. he would also pick up several boxes for his Winchester since he thought they might be needed.

By the time he got back to the livery, Cliff had the long-legged horse saddled and had a lead rope fastened to the bottom of a homemade hackamore. The boy's belongings were packed in a canvas bag sitting to one side with a bed roll laying on top. Pat noticed the butt of a Spencer rifle sticking out of his bed roll.

He climbed into the saddle and looked over to the boy. "Can you shoot that?" Quickly, the boy snapped back, "You bet I can shoot that." Before Pat rode out, he looked again at the young boy. "Bring Clayton with ya and tell him to plan on staying a while." Pat turned in the saddle, bent low and led the Crown horse out of town.

The sun was getting low when he reined in at the front of his barn. He had to unsaddle his mare and drop a fork full of hay in the manger. There she would stand as he rubbed down the tired, sweaty horse. Just then the young boy walked in and saw Pat with a cloth wiping the sweat off the gray horse. "You want me to get you a can of grain Pat?" he asked. Pat looked over and nodded. He knew what the kid wanted, "and yeah I brought your bullets.," The boy got a wide grin on his face.

Just then Pat heard Sharon calling the two for dinner. Pat walked over to a rain barrel that sat at the corner of the barn and sloshed the cool water on his face. He attempted to dry on his sleeve as he walked to the house. Josh walked at his side, Pat liked this and he liked the boy.

Dinner had been over less than an hour and Pat was sitting in a chair wiping down his rifle with a rag by the light of an oil lamp. Josh was sitting across the room doing as Pat was doing, wiping his new gun with a piece of flannel cloth. When Pat heard the approaching horse, he pulled the curtain back just a little then glanced out the window, it was dark and Pat quickly slid two rounds in the empty rifle.

Cautiously, he walked over and stood to the side of the window and gently pulled the cloth curtain aside again. In the soft light coming through the window, he could barely make out Cliff as he slid out of the saddle. He knew Cliff had brought the reply from Carl in Durango. The last time Pat was in Durango, he went to pick up Sharon. Carl was aware of this and he'd met Sharon on a couple different occasions.

Pat twisted the nob and opened the door before Cliff had had time to knock. "I got your telegram Pat. Can't stay, I gotta get back, I'm waiting on Clayton he isn't in from the Millers yet and I wanna be there with the good news," he said. Then the boy turned and sprung into the saddle and rode off into the darkness. Pat turned and stepped closer to the oil lamp that sit next to his chair.

PAT BRENNON Us Marshall

Las Animas Co.
Slaton Ranch unoccupied. As you know very secure. I will do as requested awaiting arrival. I will make all arrangements tomorrow.
Carl.

A smile came over Pat's face, this was better than he had hoped for. Pat and Jake both knew the farm, it was secluded with plenty of water close at hand. He knew Jake would be pleased. This would eliminate one of the problems, now they could concentrate on Forest

Crown and the situation with him.

It had been dark for a couple hours and Pat turned to Sharon. "This is the last chance we'll have to use the bunk house. Starting tomorrow we'll have a couple hands. The kids are asleep, so whatta ya say?" Sharon knew exactly what Pat had in mind and she liked the idea. With a smile, she moved into the bedroom and shed all her clothes. She slipped on a cotton robe then walked back into the room where Pat was waiting. There, she picked up a lantern and walked with him hand in hand to the bunkhouse.

The bunkhouse was just exactly what it was called. There was a wood stove in the middle of the floor, and five cots which were covered with cotton mattresses. The cots were fastened to the walls. It had a window at each end of the small building and rifle racks fixed to three walls. Pat and Sharon used it quite regularly as there was very little privacy with the two young ones in the main house.

The next morning, Pat finished his coffee and saddled the gray mare. With his reins in hand, he walked to the back door. Sharon pushed open the screen and stepped onto the porch letting her robe flop open. "You did that on purpose, didn't ya?" Sharon smiled big and said, "You're learning." Pat grinned and said "You might wanna pick the clothes you and the kids are gonna take with ya. If I ain't mistaken, you'll be getting on a train tomorrow," he said then he reached up and gently rubbed her leg with his hand. He then pulled himself into the saddle and headed across the open field of his Two Rivers ranch and onto the fields of the Rising Sun.

Jake was out at the corral when he thought he'd heard a horse. Turning, he saw Pat just before he reined in. Pat climbed out of the saddle and tied his reins to the corral post. Jake knew Pat was there for a reason, so he held his thought.

"What's your thoughts on getting these women out of here," Pat asked. "The way I see it, it could be a mistake keeping 'em here," Jake said. Pat agreed with a nod. "I figured on riding in today and getting tickets for them and Joe., I'm sending Joe with 'em all the way to Durango, then he can come back on the next train," Jake said. Pat agreed.

"Jake, I don't wanna put them on the train in town. I want to load 'em up on the other side of town, I don't want the folks to see them leaving in case someone says something to the wrong people. I'll ride into town and I'll be on that train. I'll stop the train when I see ya, and we'll put 'em on the train there, That way no one knows they're gone," Pat said.

Jake didn't say anything, he just smiled and agreed with the nod of his head. "I'll go in today and get their tickets," Jake said. "I have a couple new hands coming out today and I wanna square 'em off as far as what I need around the place," Pat said.

Jake looked at him curiously. "Where you find hands at?" Jake asked. "Cliff, the stable boy and his brother Clayton," Pat said. Jake smiled, "You ever see that kid ride? He rode that black and gray stud out of Saber to a stop," Jake said. "I guess his older brother can shoot a pistol. Willard told me, he spoke for Clayton and you know I do need help around there," Pat said. Then he reined around and headed back across the grass covered field.

Jake led the young horse out and snugged him up to a post and tied him off short, then gently slung a blanket over his back and topped it with a saddle. The young stallion jumped and kicked a little before he settled down. He reminded him of Saber. Saber had done the same thing when Jake first broke him. The more resistance the young stallion showed the more Jake liked him. This young horse was Saber all over again and Jake couldn't be more pleased with the young horse. Jake then gently reached down and pulled the cinch up and strung it through the buckle. He was surprised when the horse showed no resistance.

Once saddled, Jake walked back into the house and took three of the double eagles and slid 'em into his pocket. "I'm getting you out of here early tomorrow morning. Joe will be going to Durango with you and Sharon. Everything is arranged," Jake said.

Jake went back to the waiting horse, carefully he slipped his toe in the stirrup and swung his leg over, expecting the usual objection from the three-year-old. But to his surprise the horse just side stepped a little and settled down.

Softly, he touched him with his spurs and the horse obeyed as though he wanted to go. *Just like his dad* Jake thought. Jake smiled and set a pace for the back field where he knew Joe and Web were pulling wire.

When he rode up to the boys, he saw they had burlap wrapped around their gloved hands. Joe was wearing his pistol; Web was shirtless and wasn't wearing a gun. When Jake started to leave, he noticed there was only one rifle in the wagon. "Whose Winchester is that?" he asked. "It's mine Jake, the one Pat loaned me," Joe said. Jake looked at Web, "I know you own a Colt pistol and a Winchester. You don't go unarmed anymore, I'm expecting trouble and I'm gonna need both of ya," Jake said. He didn't take the time to explain what was going on, he would let them know later exactly what the situation was.

Jake had to get in and out of town because he had things at the ranch that had to be Done and he wasn't comfortable leaving Jodie alone. Web reached in his pocket, pulled out two silver dollars and walked up to Jake and handed 'em to him. "Jake, will you pick me up a box of forty-fives and a box of forty-four forty's' while you're in town?" Jake agreed with a nod, now he knew why Web wasn't armed.

Jake touched his spurs to the horse and the

two boys watched him fade into the green fields of the ranch. It wasn't but a couple hours and Jake rode up to the train station and climbed out of the saddle. He stepped through the door and the smell of pipe smoke hit him in the face. There behind the counter with that pipe hanging out of his mouth stood Chester, chewing on the end of that pipe.

Jake walked up to the little old man who glanced back at him over the tops of his glasses. "What can I do for you Jake?" he asked. "I'll be needing five tickets to Durango on tomorrow's train, one of which will be round trip." The little old man reached in the shallow drawer and produced the yellow paper tickets, one he stamped with a round trip label. "I'm betting these are hush-hush aren't they Jake," he asked. Jake took the tickets and nodded in agreement and headed for the mercantile.

He walked in and was warmly greeted by the clerk, Grace Miller. Jake had grown up with her and her brothers of which there were five. "I need some bullets, Grace. Give me four boxes of those forty-fives and three boxes of those forty-four forties and a box of those thirty-eight rim fires," he said as he pointed high up on a shelf. He knew Jodie always traveled with a small pistol so he laid in a box of the thirty-eight RF just in case.

"It looks like you might be having a little trouble, Jake. Remember, if you need help, me and my brothers will be there," she said as she stacked the bullets on the counter. This made Jake feel good, he didn't have to be told, he knew the Millers and he knew he could count on them. As Jake started to leave, the friendly clerk said, "You be careful, Jake Cleary." Jake nodded and smiled as he went through the door. He then dumped the boxes of bullets in his saddle bags and mounted up.

The ride back gave him time to think and make plans for what was coming. The one thing he knew for sure, the one he treasured most would be safe.

He wasn't far from Pat's place when he saw a nice looking red and white yearling calf not more than fifty yards off the wagon road. Jake reined to the right and calmly threw a loop over her. The calf bawled and pulled and did everything to escape the rope to no avail. Jake took up a little slack and pulled the stubborn calf through the gate of Pat's Two Rivers ranch. The house sat a good five hundred yards beyond the gate. From there he could see Pat standing watching him drag the stubborn calf down the narrow road.

Seeing the calf in tow Pat knew it was Jake and set his rifle down. When he got close, Pat asked. "Where'd you get her?" Just then Clayton stepped out of the barn. Jake noticed he was wearing a Colt on his hip. Pat turned to Clayton. "You go find out where she got out and you get Cliff and fix the hole," Pat said. Jake moved forward a little and tossed the pistol wearing ranch hand the rope. "By the way Clayton, he's Jake Cleary. He has full run of the place; his spread connects with mine." "Pleased to meet you Mr. Cleary, I've seen you around, I'm Clayton Raynes." "Call me Jake, Clayton. I ain't old enough to be called Mr. Cleary. The boy smiled and pulled the calf into the corral.

He climbed out of the saddle and walked to where Pat stood in the shade. "I'll be by early in the morning with the wagon. You can leave your horse at the livery. After you get off the train, you can take Joe's horse back to town and leave it in the stable, he'll be needing it when he gets back from Durango," Jake said. Pat nodded in agreement and said, "You care for a drink?" Jake smiled and the two walked into the barn where Pat had a bottle of whisky sitting on a corner shelf above a few sacks of grain along with several boxes of bullets. Jake took a mouth full and once again climbed into the saddle and cut a trail across the field to his house.

CHAPTER

4

Two hours before sunup Jake slipped on his boots. He could smell the coffee and he wasn't at all surprised to see he wasn't the first one up. Jodie had a fire in the stove and coffee brewing. Before he could stop to eat, he had to hook up a team to the wagon and throw hay for the horses that were corralled he had two prize pregnant mares that were close to birthing, those in the pastures were on their own.

When he walked into the kitchen Jodie was rolling out dough on a flat kitchen board. Her raven black hair was held back with flowered pins keeping it off her shoulders. He had never had such a life before he married her and he was grateful. She smiled when he walked in and picked up her cup, taking a sip of the steaming brew. As he set it down, he gently patted her lightly on the back.

As he left, he was careful not to slam the

screen door this early in the morning. He knew Jodie hated hearing the screen door slam. He was buttoning his shirt as he stepped off the porch. "Everybody up," he hollered knowing Joe and Web would hear him. Soon he saw the dim yellow light in the bunk house start to grow.

They had at least three horses to saddle one of them the fidgeting three-year-old that never made the job easy. These two hands could saddle and bridle a horse as quick as most people got dressed. These were some of the everyday chores that had to happen before breakfast seven days a week. Jake had a rule at the ranch, there always must be a mount saddled and ready to ride without fail. Web, being the newest hand, inherited this chore the day he hired in.

By the time the horses were saddled and the wagon hitched up, the smell of biscuits and coffee led them to the table. Joe, web and Jake sat down at the dining room table Jodie had brought with her from Cripple Creek. They loved having a meal they didn't have to eat out of a skillet and coffee that didn't come with grounds . "This will be the last one for a while, now you boys are on your own as far as the cooking goes,"

Jodie said. Joe and Web sighed a little but remained silent, they knew this situation would be uncomfortable, but it wasn't permanent and it had to be for now. Jake put on his hat and picked up his rifle and the two hands followed him out the door to the waiting wagon.

It was dark and the only light was that of a lantern he had set on the porch. By the dim light Jake slid his rifle into the scabbard that was tied to his saddle. Jodie stepped onto the porch and dropped her small pistol into her handbag, then Jake helped her onto the wagon next to Joe.

Joe had his horse tied to the back of the wagon, he knew he was driving and he knew approximately where he would meet the train. Web had already climbed into the saddle. Today he wore the Colt pistol he took off the horse thief that was trying to kill him, and he had the same man's Winchester tucked in his scabbard.

"Don't cut across, take the road to Pat's," Jake said. With a slap of the reins the wagon began to roll. In less than an hour Sharon was sitting next to Jodie and the two kids were in the back of the wagon. Jake and Pat rode in front of the team, setting a quick pace, while Web rode alongside the wagon. It was seven in the morning when Joe reined left and headed toward the town of LasAnimas. When the buildings come into view, Joe pulled the team left to stay out of sight as much as possible.

Pat rode into town and directly to the livery stable just as though today was just like any other day. He dismounted and led the white eyed mare into one of the rear stalls. Before he could get the cinch unbuckled, he heard a voice over his shoulder say, "You want me to strip that saddle, Marshall." Pat turned to see the new hostler standing several feet away holding a brush. Pat didn't recognize him but he did look familiar.

He was maybe six foot tall and solid built, Pat guessed him to be in his early thirties. He wore his dark brown hair long enough to touch his shoulders. He didn't wear brogans like most hostlers, he wore boots. His long sideburns come down and met under his chin, making a short beard. Pat didn't know where, but he was sure he had seen him somewhere.

Pat noticed he wasn't wearing a hat or a gun, but he was wearing a white handled knife on his side which was common for a hostler. Pat looked around but didn't see a pistol or a rifle anywhere. *Maybe he doesn't wear a gun*, Pat thought.

"I'm Pat Brennon," he said as he reached out to shake his hand. The hostler returned the gesture. "I'm Levi Boone, pleased to meet you marshal," he said as they shook hands. Pat noticed he had a grip; he could tell this guy was a working hand. Still, Pat was a little puzzled. "Naw I'm just gonna take this saddle off for a while and let her cool," Pat said.

Pat pulled his rifle out of the scabbard and headed for the small café where he would wait for the whistle to tell him the train to Durango was nearby. He walked in and as usual dropped down at a corner table with his back to the wall, his Winchester at his fingertips standing in the corner.

He didn't have to order; the waitress knew Pat and she knew he was there to sip coffee. From there he could watch the main street.

Jake signaled Joe and he pulled the team to a stop a little more than a mile beyond town. At this distance they could faintly hear the whistle scream. The two kids immediately jumped out of the wagon and pressed their ears to the track to see if they could hear the train coming their way.

Jodie and Sharon climbed down to stretch their legs. "I hate that wagon bench," Jodie said as she stretched her back. "It definitely needs a pad or pillow," Sharon said with a giggle. Jake and Web climbed out of the saddle to give the horses a slight break. Joe rifle in hand, stood up and looked around.

Hearing the whistle, Pat dropped a piece of silver on the table as he picked up his rifle. Stepping onto the boardwalk, he looked around a little then started the walk to the water tower where he knew engine number 40 would come to rest. When he got there, he stepped into the shadow of the leaking tank. He moved to one side a little to avoid the small leak and to protect his rifle, then he pinned his badge to his shirt and waited.

There wasn't a breeze in the air and Pat could see and smell the smoke a half mile off. The engineer had no idea what was about to happen, nobody did but Jake and Joe. Patiently, he waited for the black coal burner to roll to a stop.

As the fireman pulled the water trough

down, water splashed over the top of the engine, wetting the toes of Pat's boots. From where they stood, Jake, Jodie and Sharon could now see the smoke of the engine a mile in the distance.

The two kids were excited, they had never ridden on a train before and this was a big day for them. Jake, holding the reins in his hand, led the antsy young horse to the far side of the wagon and tied the lead rope off short. He wasn't taking the chance of the young horse spooking and running off.

When the fireman raised the trough, Pat stepped out of the shadows and climbed into the engine compartment with the engineer. When the engineer and the fireman saw the badge, they greeted Pat with a "Hello Marshall, you going with us?" "Part way," Pat answered. The engineer looked back, waiting for the signal to move. When it came, he gently pulled back on the throttle and the black smoker begin to roll forward.

As the speed begin to increase, Pat looked at the engineer and said, "Keep it down, you're gonna make a quick stop up here a short piece to take on some passengers." The dust covered engineer looked at him with question.

Just then Pat gestured with his head telling the engineer to look forward. In the distance he saw the wagon, several people and three horses. "They're getting on." Then he looked at the fireman, his face and clothes were covered with black coal dust as was the engineer's. "I would appreciate it if you boys kept this to yourselves," Pat said. The nervous fireman said, "Ok Marshall." The engineer who knew Pat well agreed with a nod.

"Marshall, I think the second car back is empty," the engineer said. Pat gave him a slight nod and smiled. The dust covered engineer knew this was law business and he knew the US Marshall. The black faced engineer slowly pushed the handle forward and the train begin to slow.

"I'll pull her to a stop where the second car back is right in front of 'em," he said with an air of certainty. When the wheels stopped turning, he looked at Pat and grinned. "I told ya," he said. Pat nodded at him and said. "You sure did." As soon as the train came to rest, Pat jumped out of the engine compartment and Joe jumped off the wagon. Rifle in hand, he took the three steps up into the waiting car, set his rifle down, then jumped to the ground. Without a word he picked up Josh and set him down at the top of the stairs, then he lifted the girl. "Go take any seat you want," he said. Both kids laughed and ran down the aisle of the empty car.

Jodie stepped up and Jake handed her a small leather bag. "There's three hundred gold in there," he said, then gently kissed her and watched her walk into the car. Pat walked with Sharon to the edge of the train, and before she stepped up, he opened her handbag and dropped a dozen double eagles in and pulled the tie cords shut. He then bent over slightly and kissed her and said, "Don't worry."

She smiled a little and a tear came to her eye. It was a little past eight in the morning when the wheels began to turn on an eleven-hour trip to Durango Colorado.

Jake looked at Web and gave him a nod telling him to drive the wagon. The young boy climbed out of the saddle, tied his horse to the back, then climbed on and took the reins. Pat walked up to Joe's horse and slid his rifle into the scabbard and mounted up. "Take the wagon back to the ranch. We won't be far behind," Jake said.

Web slapped the reins on the horses back and turned the wagon around and rode in his own tracks. Jodie took a seat facing the rear of the car next to an open window. As the train slowly began to roll, Jodie, with a tear in her eye, reached out the window and waved. Jake and Pat sat mounted and watched the train roll out of sight "I'll feel better with them gone," Jake said. They then rode into town as they had done many times, this time to see the sheriff.

As they came into town Jake reined to the sheriff's office while Pat rode directly to the livery stable. There, he stabled Joe's horse and stripped the horse of saddle and bridle, then picked up a gunny sack that hung over a stall and wiped the sweat of the horse. He dumped a small can of oats in the manger.

Just then the new hostler walked up to where Pat was saddling his mare. "Joe will be back the next day or two, so keep his horse fed and grained," Pat said, then he handed the man two silver dollars.

Reins in hand, he led his mare to the sheriff's office. When he walked in Jake was there giving Willard the rundown on Forest Crown. "Willard, you know what you're looking for, so if you see anyone that fits the picture, you keep out of it. These are professional gunman and a badge to them is no more than a target, so if they come looking for the Marshall, you just send them out to my place and act like you know nothing," Pat said.

With these words, they both left the office and stepped into the hot sun. Just as they started to mount up, the clatter of a wagon caught their attention. When they looked around, they saw Web driving right down the middle of the road heading for home. He waved and smiled as a kid would do. Jake grinned a little and Pat pointed to him, then they tapped their mounts and rode past the wagon and the boy. "Pat, we haven't got any idea where Crown is and no way to find out until he makes a move," Jake said as they rode. "We're surely in a pickle," Pat replied. When they reached Pat's entry road they reined their mounts to a slow, walk to Pat's barn.

"We just gotta wait until something happens Pat, I don't like it but we have no choice," Jake said. "Oh yeah Pat, I forgot to tell ya.

You remember that Winchester we got off Delaney that you told Joe to take care of for ya a couple years past?" Pat answered with a nod. "Well, I sold it to him for twenty-five dollars a couple months back and spent the money," Jake said, then he laughed and set his spurs beating a trail across the grass field. Pat sit there a few seconds and started to laugh then climbed out of the saddle.

CHAPTER

5

The two women had been sitting on the hard bench for nearly eleven hours. The two young one's tired and irritable stretched out on an empty seat and slept off and on throughout the tedious trip. Joe sat behind them holding his Winchester, occasionally walking up and down the narrow aisle to stretch his legs. The ladies had put together a basket of food for the trip and hadn't left the train since they climbed aboard.

Jodie had just started to doze when the whistle screamed signaling the end to a eleven-hour trip and raising her out of the nap she almost got. Joe was glad the trip was over, but he knew he would be making a return trip the next day.

In the black of night, the train rolled into Durango. All that could be seen were the well-lit saloons and a single lamp burning in front of the train station. Just as the car they rode in slowly passed the single lamp, Joe saw a man leaning against a wood front building, then he saw the quick reflection off the badge he wore. Sharon was busy helping the young ones put on their shoes and gather up sweaters. As Jodie stared out the window, she saw the same badge.

Joe stepped off the train first and helped the tired kids to the ground. Sharon followed the kids and was immediately approached by the man and the badge. As Carl walked up to Sharon, Joe walked to her side, his rifle in hand. When he greeted her, he took off his hat before he spoke. "Miss Sharon, it's good to see you again. Everything has been arranged," Carl said as he was putting his hat back on. Just then Jodie walked up carrying her canvas bag. Again, Carl politely removed his hat. "You must be Jodie," he said.

Jodie put out her hand as a greeting. "As I was telling Miss Sharon, you have three rooms at the hotel tonight. I have a wagon; in the morning I will take you back out to the ranch. By the way, how are Pat and Jake?" Carl asked, then he looked at Joe. "You might wanna check inside to see when the train heads back your way," Carl said. Joe turned and did as the sheriff suggested. When he walked through the door, he saw what looked like the clerk napping behind the desk. When he left, he knew his eleven-hour ride back to Las Animas left at roughly at eight am.

After a good night's sleep, Jodie and Sharon met in the hall. Sharon took Josh by the hand and Jodie took Emily and the four walked down the stairs. "There's a café a couple doors down, we can get something to eat there Jodie," Sharon said.

When they walked into the little café with the two kids in hand, they saw Joe sitting at a table near the window; he was waiting for the train he could not and would not miss. Seeing them walk in, he stood and waited for them to be seated. In the middle of the table sat a gray porcelain coffee pot, a small cloud of steam slowly drifted upward, filling the air with the smell of fresh coffee.

Jodie looked at the pot and smiled when she smelled the coffee, then said "good" in a low soft tone. As it worked out, Sharon sat next to the window and looked down the street in a town she once knew. As she stared, memories filled her mind. Durango was a town full of good and bad memories for her. She remembered when she first met Pat and Jake and what circumstances brought about that meeting. Her husband and the father of her two kids was murdered by a gambler. Before his body was home, Pat and Jake, hung the gambler for that murder.

They hadn't been seated long when the waitress returned with an arm load of plates filled with biscuits and white gravy. "I knew you'd be hungry and who doesn't like biscuits and gravy," Joe asked. The only other words spoken was a pleasant thank you to the waitress. As the two young ones finished their breakfast, a beautiful black horses pulled a covered two-seat buckboard to the front of the café.

The small usually empty space Behind the back seat had a stiff paper box and a half full burlap bag leaving only enough room for the two bags the ladies brought. Carl had his horse saddled and tied to the back of the wagon.

Before Carl could get down and into the café, the whistle Joe had been waiting for, screamed, letting him know the boring eleven-hour trip he didn't look forward to was at hand.

Once Carl stepped into the café, Joe got to his feet and dropped a five-dollar gold coin on the table. Carl walked up and Joe shook his hand. "Pleased to have met you Carl, they're all yours now. I know you'll take care of 'em," he said. Carl nodded to Joe and asked the ladies if they were ready to go. Jodie dropped her napkin on the table and Sharon took a last sip of the coffee. Then the two ladies calmly walked to the wagon following the two anxious kids.

Joe had no luggage, all he brought was a Winchester rifle, a Colt pistol, a canteen, and a pair of leather saddle bags. In those he carried a knife, and a small amount of ammunition for the guns.

The stink of burning coal filled his nose as he walked towards the train. When he got closer to the engine, it blew a blast of steam just before the conductor hollered all aboard and then the whistle again sounded. Joe stepped onto the stairs at the back of the third car from the engine.

He looked into the empty car and dropped down in a seat against the back wall, then he dropped his saddlebags in an empty seat facing him. Joe was tired so he leaned back in the corner and pulled his hat down over his eyes. With a sharp jerk, the train slowly began to roll and he quietly drifted off into the sleep he missed the night before.

He awoke with the conductor tapping on the back of the seat in front of him. When he lifted his hat, he saw the old man holding a shiny paper punch in his hand. "I know you have a ticket, I just gotta punch a hole in it. I got off number 40 in Durango last night same as you did, now I'm like you riding 99 back to Las Animas."

Joe yawned and pulled his ticket out of his shirt pocket and handed it to the friendly old man as he dropped down in the seat in front of him. After he handed back the ticket he reached into his pocket and produced a small bottle of whiskey and tipped it back. "I've shared many a sip with Pat as we rode these rails," then he handed the near empty bottle to Joe.

To Joe this was like a gift, he looked into the bottle a second then tipped it back, making sure he didn't finish it. "You got manners boy. Just like Pat," the old man said, then he drained what was left and threw the bottle out the window. Joe smiled and said thanks.

Sharon and Jodie were sitting on each side of Emily in the back seat while Josh with his new rifle set up front with Carl. Sharon never spoke as they rode out of Durango and Jodie knew returning to where the two young ones were born and where she buried her husband had to be so very hard so Jodie left her to the privacy of her own thoughts. When the buckboard rolled around the final curve before they got to the house, Sharon asked carl to stop.

There over five hundred yards in the distance set the ranch house she occupied and loved for nearly nine years. When she and Pat left, she thought she'd never see this place again. When they came to a stop, both kids shouted, "mommy we're home". Hearing this brought tears to Sharon's eyes. She looked at Jodie with a tear in her eye and softly said, "so many memories." Jodie put her arm around her and said, "It'll be alright the kids now have two homes, they'll enjoy it." "We can go now Carl," Jodie said.

Carl clicked the horse forward and they drove the last little bit to the front door where Carl reined in. Before he could get down, Josh jumped off the the wagon with his rifle in hand. "Ms. Jodie, I brought a half dozen chickens out here yesterday and I have enough grub in the back of the wagon to last you a few days. I'll leave the wagon here for you so you'll have a way into town if need be," Carl said. Then Sharon stepped through the front door. "Thank you, Carl you've been a big help I know Jake would thank you if he was here," Jodie said.

Jodie grabbed the two bags and walked into the empty farmhouse while Sharon stood and looked around. The house not being occupied for this length of time had collected a thick layer of gray dust on everything. Carl walked in behind Jodie and dropped the provisions near the kitchen. "I'll go unhitch the buckboard and stable the horse now, Mrs. Brennon, and I'll get you some ready firewood before I leave," he said. Both women thanked him as he walked out.

"We're lucky Sharon all the windows have glass in them and we have a stove in the kitchen and mattresses on the beds," Jodie said. Sharon broke her stare and walked back into the kitchen she left behind more than a year ago. Just then the sound of a double bitted ax ripping through a log reminded her of the first time Pat and Jake come to the house.

"I'll bet if you look in that cabinet, you'll find an old coffee pot and an oil lamp," Sharon said. Jodie walked up and stood on her tip toes to reach the porcelain pot then once again on her toes to reached the lamp. She held it next to her ear and jiggled it to see if it still had oil.

"We have oil in the lamp and we're gonna have coffee in a few minutes," she said. Hearing this seemed to change Sharon's mood a little. Just then Josh walked in with his rifle in his hand. "Josh, I want you to put the rifle down and go to the windmill and fill the coffee pot all the way to the top for me," Jodie said. Josh smiled and leaned his twenty-two against the wall and took the pot from Jodie and let the screen door slam behind him.

Carl with an arm load of split firewood pulled the door open and dumped the kindling next to the stove. There's more out there, nothing too big for Josh to handle. I'll be back tomorrow with some hay for the horse and anything else I can think of. O yeah, I put some pans and plates and cups in there yesterday," he said as he pointed to the cabinet next to the stove. Jodie opened her handbag and took out one of the double eagles Jake had given her and offered it to Carl.

"Carl when you come back will you bring a few more lamps and a can of oil and maybe some coffee," Jodie asked. Carl put up a restraining hand rejecting the coin then spoke. "You keep your money Ms. Jodie I can easily round all that up without it, I wouldn't like myself much if I took your money," he said. Then he turned and climbed on his horse and rode away.

The old conductor flipped open the face of his watch and quickly glanced at it, "We'll be coming into Canon City in about hour and a half," he said then he snapped the watch closed. Joe knew after that it was Salida then La Junta and then Las Animas and back to the ranch, and the place he called home.

It was afternoon and Joe squirmed a little sitting on the hard bench. The only thing he could do was stare out the window at the sea of passing sage- brush. After hours of boredom, he pulled his Colt and wiped it down with his bandana, then he drug a rag through the cylinder as he did the barrel.

Then the train came around the long curve he had been waiting for and began its run alongside the Arkansas River. Joe knew Canon City was close. He was hungry, the ladies had brought sandwiches the day before, but he had never given food any thought for the trip back and he was starved.

He had taken this run the day before and he knew they would be in Canon long enough for him to grab something to eat and just maybe a drink of whiskey. He sat and stared out the window as the train slowly rolled past the high stone wall of the territory's most notorious penitentiary. He didn't have to wait long before the whistle sung and the train began to slow.

As it slowly rolled towards the station, he saw six men and three horses standing a few yards back from the tracks waiting for the train to stop. The one thing he noticed was five of these men were armed and had their guns tied down. He remembered Jake saying, "Keep an eye open." Just then the hair on the back of his neck stood up. Before the train came to rest, he was waiting at the top of the three stairs.

The wheels hadn't completely stopped when Joe stepped off the stairs onto the platform with his rifle in hand. The ticket office and telegraph were at his left, but he turned right: he had to have a better look at the men that captured his attention. He was as close as ten yards away when one of the horses whinnied and reared up, causing the others to spook and bolt in all directions.

That is when Joe saw the Crown brand burned onto the hip of one of the horses. Jake had told him and Web the whole story and what was going on. One of the gunman holding the reins tried to get control and settle them down.

Joe knew then who the man in the fine suit was. Trying not to draw any attention to himself, he nonchalantly looked away, then turned and headed into the town.

After all he saw he knew he needed to send a wire. Once on the main street of Canon City he turned left and headed back toward the train station. He knew exactly where his destination was. As he walked, he saw on the opposite side of the street the word café painted on a glass window. *That will have to wait,* he thought. Just past a building he saw to be a laundry, he again turned and headed for the tracks.

When he stepped into the open, he looked to see the three horses being loaded into a cattle car. Now three of the men he could no longer see, he knew were loading horses. Being there were only three passenger cars, he thought, *this bunch won't be hard to find.*

Joe moving quickly stepped up onto the platform and walked into the ticket office. In the back of the office, he could hear the telegraph key clicking. When he walked up to the counter in front of the clicking key and saw a bald -headed man looking down tapping out a message to someone, somewhere down the line.

When the clerk looked up, he saw an impatient young man watching him like a hawk. "What can I do for you young man," he asked. "I have to send a wire to Las Animas, to the US Marshall, and it is confidential," Joe replied. The bald man picked up a pencil and said, "what would you like to say?" he asked.

"To Pat Brennon U. S. Marshall
Las Animas Co.

Six coming your way. Sign it, Joe Burk and I need it sent now," he said.

The man behind the counter looked up and said, "that'll be one dollar." Joe reached in his pocket and handed him the coin, only then did the teller begin to tap on the brass key. After a few seconds he looked at Joe and said, "Sent." Joe smiled and left the office and headed for the window that said café.

He made his way back to the main street and the window with the friendly invitation. His rifle still in hand he walked into the little café, instantly the soft smell of bread or biscuits, he really couldn't tell which with a hint of coffee filled his nose making him even more hungry. He hadn't smelled anything but the stink of burning coal since he left Durango. He smiled slightly then dropped down at the closest table and laid his rifle across the top. He looked around to discover he was alone except for a freckle faced red-headed waitress.

To Joe she looked as though she was fresh out of school. Pleasantly, she walked up to Joe, who was waiting with a smile. "And what can I get you sir?" she asked. "What have you got I can have right now?" he asked, "Can you make me a couple sandwiches? I'm kind of in a rush, I can't miss that train you hear puffing."

Quickly, she glanced up toward the tracks. "How about a roast beef sandwich?" she answered. "I'll take two and can you wrap 'em up so I can take 'em with me?" he asked. The young girl turned and walked back into the kitchen. It was but a couple minutes and she returned with a package wrapped in what looked to be newsprint.

He reached back into his pocket and brought out the last coin he had and handed it to her. "Will this cover it, it's all I got?" he asked. She looked at the dollar and smiled. "Yes sir that will cover it," she answered, and he took the newsprint, and picked up his rifle and headed back to the tracks. The young waitress walked to the window and watched the boy she had never seen before walk away.

With his rifle in one hand and a package of food in the other Joe casually walked down the platform glancing up at the windows as he passed. There in the second car he saw the face of the man dressed in the fine suit. Crown looked down at him as he walked by.

As though he saw nothing, he walked to the far end of the third car where his canteen and saddle bags waited. For now, the most important thing was the sandwiches the red headed waitress made and wrapped for him. As soon as he sit, he pulled the cork on his canteen and folded back the newspaper and started eating.

While he was enjoying the last of the beef sandwich the whistle once more sounded followed by a sharp jerk and the train began to roll. Just then, the back door swung open and two well-armed men carrying Winchester rifles looked at him as they walked up the narrow isle and into the middle car. Joe tipped the canteen and washed down what he thought was the best sandwich he ever had eaten.

He rolled up the newspaper in a tight ball and tossed it out the open window. Just then the conductor came through the door. "How much longer to Las Animas?" he asked. "Salida is next then La junta and Las Animas. be about three hours," he answered and kept walking.

It was late afternoon and Joe knew he would have a horse waiting and he would ride back to the ranch in the dark to tell Jake all he had seen. For now, he stretched his legs across to the facing seat and was going to try to get some sleep if he could.

He awoke out of a sound sleep he so desperately needed to the sound of the whistle howling. He sat up and yawned. He tipped the canteen once more. As the train slowed, he stared out the window and watched the well-lit station come into view. Once the train was at rest, Joe stepped off and into the darkness in between two cars.

As he looked around, he saw three men step out of the middle car. Two of the men walked with the man, he thought to be Crown to a buckboard and a couple saddled horses. *Now why would he get off in La junta, it is only fifteen miles from Las Animas. Why here?* He thought.

Now that leaves three of 'em still on the train. Jakes gonna want to know this, he thought.

Joe stepped back out of the shadows and into the car. He couldn't sleep anymore, now all he had on his mind was to get off this train.

He was fed up with this ride. He was tired of the constant clicking of the wheels on the tracks and hard bench and just the ride itself. The last hour between La Junta and Llas Animas seemed like it would never end. When he heard the whistle scream, he grabbed his gear, and stepped in-between the cars and waited at the top of the three stairs.

Before the train completely stopped, he made a quick step down and onto the platform. With his saddlebags over one shoulder and his canteen hanging off the other he walked rifle in hand away from the train yard and directly to the livery stable.

It was at least eight o'clock and the night was blacker than coal, he knew at this hour no one saw him leave the train. Moving at a rush he went into the livery and touched a match to the oil lamp hanging just inside. He knew it wouldn't be long and he would be joined by the three men that rode in the second car.

Quickly, he saddled his horse and tied on his

bags and leaped into the saddle. As he passed the oil lamp, he snuffed the flame and rode out of the livery stable and into the dark of night. Once out of the wood building, he rode across the street and waited.

He didn't have long to wait when he heard, before he saw, the three horses being led down the back street to the front of the stable. That's all he wanted. He knew now the gunmen were checking in. Seeing this, he turned and set his horse to a constant trot.

CHAPTER

6

Without the moon there was total darkness; he had to rely on his sense of direction and his horse to get him back to the ranch. Once there, he would tell Jake of all he knew and had seen. He guessed it to be close to ten o'clock when he saw off to his right a dim yellow light. Now he knew exactly where he was. He had ridden past the entrance to Pat's ranch and was approaching the place he called home. He didn't have to turn his horse, the mare followed in the trail she had followed countless times.

As soon as Joe's boots were on the ground, he heard the squeak of the screen door, a sound he had heard numerous times over the years. "It's me Jake," he said. Just then, a yellow light began to grow on the back porch and he again heard the screen door. After he unsaddled and stabled his mount he walked to the light. Before he walked in, he picked up the lantern and carried it back into the house.

"How was your trip, Joe?" Jake asked. Joe set the oil burner on the table and turned up the wick to a higher flame. There sat Jake with a bottle of rye, two empty glasses and his Colt. Joe picked up a glass and dropped down into the chair across the table. Jake leaned over and poured the small glass to the rim then he filled his.

"If I ever ride another train, it'll be too soon, I couldn't get off quick enough," he answered. Jake laughed. "It ain't so bad in the cattle car where you can stretch out," he said.

"I saw the telegram, you sure it was Crown?" Jake asked. "I think so, this guy wasn't young and he wore a fine suit, oh yeah, he wore a watch chain, it had some kind of a gold bauble hanging on it. I couldn't see for sure what it was, and I wasn't going to stare." Joe answered. Then he went on. "I didn't tell you, he got off the train with two of his men in La Junta. I saw there was a couple horses and a buckboard waiting on him."

Jake's eyes narrowed slightly when he

heard gold bauble, he then pretty much knew Joe was right. "He kept two men with 'em when he got off the train, you say." Joe finished the small drink and was refilling his glass while he answered yes with a nod.

"You go on to the bunk house and get some sleep, first light I'm riding to Pats. He thinks there are five so I'll let him know," Jake said. Joe got to his feet, when he stepped onto the back porch, he picked up his bags and faded into the dark. Jake sat a minute then carried the oil burner into the empty bedroom.

Jake was awake and on his feet before sunup as always. He reached over and set a match to the oil lamp that sat on a small table. Barefooted, he carried the lamp into the kitchen and started pumping the pump handle to fill the coffee pot. He realized he hadn't done this since Jodie moved in with him. He glanced up to see a dim light in the bunk house from the kitchen window and he knew in a very few minutes he would have company around the table.

It was but a couple minutes when he heard the squeak of the screen and the sound of boots on the porch. Without saying a word, Web walked over and started filling the firebox with kindling. Joe handed him a small can of lamp oil and he splashed it inside the firebox and tossed in a match. He set the pot over an open hole. Quietly, all three sat and waited for the coffee.

Jake sat down in the leather chair and started pulling on his boots, when he noticed Joe and Web were both armed. He looked at Joe, "Is there anything you can tell me about the men you saw?" He asked. Waiting for the coffee to boil, Joe yawned and answered.

"There wasn't much light on that train, but I did notice the rig one of them wore. It was a short cut holster that was fastened to the belt at an angle where it looked like it was leaning back and the muzzle was pointing a little forward. Now that I think of it there weren't any bullet loops on the belt and had tassels hanging off the tops of his boots. I don't know which one, but at least one of them is riding the Crown brand."

Jake could hear and smell the coffee boiling. Not saying anything he walked over and got three metal cups and tossed them across the room to Joe and Web. There they sat in silence sipping coffee that was too hot and waiting for the rise of the sun. It was dark and quiet this early, the only sound was the crowing of a rooster somewhere in the yard.

"You boys don't leave the ranch, everything as normal but you stick around the house and keep your rifles close at hand. If you see anyone coming you don't know, don't let them near the house," Jake said. They both nodded in agreement and sipped their coffee.

Jake walked over and pulled the curtain aside to look out the window for a second. "I'm gonna head over to Pats and let him know what's changed." Jake then walked to the barn and started to saddling the temperamental young stallion. Once he had him cinched down tight, he slowly climbed into the saddle. The young horse bucked a couple times then settled down and bent to Jake's command.

Jake, atop the long-legged horse, touched him with his heels and ran across the open fields and into Pat's back yard, never slowing down. When Jake rode up, Pat was pitching hay into a manger inside the corral, as always, his rifle as always was at his fingertips. Jake climbed down and relayed to him what Joe had told him.

"I don't think they're stupid enough to ride out here," Jake said, then he went on. "We gotta go into town and you know it same as I do, so let's go get this done on our terms: quick and final," Jake said.

Pat reached in his saddlebags and pulled out the Colt pistol he kept but seldom used and flipped the gate open then dropped in six of the big bullets. "I keep this unloaded with Josh around, you can't never tell what a kid will do," Pat said.

Jake checked the fill in his pistol and climbed back into the saddle. Just then Cliff and Clayton came around the corner. "We're going into town, no one should be coming out here, don't let anyone get within pistol range," Pat said, then he spurred the white eyed mare and rode out of sight with Jake at his side.

Their ride was silent, they knew they were going up against hardened hired gunman, gunmen that would be more than glad to shoot you in the back to earn their bounty. Crown didn't hire second best and they both knew it. Pat wasn't a pistoleer; he was a rifleman and there were few better, but these men were artists with a six-shooter. They were men of the gun.

Now, Jake was at home with a hand full of iron, but he would need an edge when he faced the guns hired by Forest Crown. He spent a lot of time on the trail chasing bounty. Now he had a bounty on his own head and he didn't like it.

He knew if they were good enough and lucky enough, he and Pat just might ride away from this unscathed. He hadn't even seen the men that hunted him but that was soon to change.

It was a fifteen-mile ride and little was said, Pat rode at Jake's side. Both men rode with a twinge of fear because they had yet to see the enemy. *His holster leaning back barrel pointed forward.* This thought rode every step with Jake. He had never seen a rig like this. Pat didn't like being put in a position where he had to use a pistol, but these worries were normal for men like Jake and Pat because they too were men of the gun.

At the first sight of town, Jake reined in, Pat pulled around facing him. "We have very few options Pat, we know they're here and why. I don't like being hunted, now they're the ones being hunted," Jake said. Pat turned his horse and looked at the town in the distance.

"They're looking for the red-headed marshal, they don't know what I look like, so I'll find them. They won't even know they're being hunted," Jake said. "How you figure, what you got in mind Jake?" Pat asked. "We'll go to the stable and you wait for me there. Once I find 'em I'll come get you," Jake said. Pat grinned and nodded then they headed for the back street and the stable.

They touched their horses and moved steady. They now had some sort of a plan but they still didn't know who they were looking for. When they got close, they reined around the end of town trying to keep out of sight as much as possible. Arriving at the livery, they both leaned down in the saddle and rode through the low door. The first thing they saw once inside were two horses carrying the Crown brand.

What they didn't know was, they were being watched from the upstairs window at the hotel. That hotel ran from Front Street to Back street like most all buildings in town. The windows in the upstairs afforded a view of the Back street.

The livery stable was too the left of the hotel and down nearly sixty yards. While Chuck Meeks strapped his Colt around his waist, he watched Jake and Pat lean low in the saddle and ride into the stable. "Well, well, look at this Harv," Chuck said. Harv Collins, who shared a room with Meeks, walked over to the window and looked down at the livery stable.

"I don't see anything," he said. "Our red headed marshall and his friend just rode in," Meeks added, then turned from the window leaving Harv watching the stable. "Look at this Chuck," Harv said. Chuck turned back to the window and watched their companion and fellow gunman walk into the stable alone. "Arch has got 'em in the stable, he might need some help, Chuck said.

The two men quickly left the room. Collins was buckling on his shoulder holster as the door closed behind him. Mary, who was behind the desk, watched as the two men quickly descended the stairs and hurried out the door.

This livery stable had four rows of stalls, two running down the middle facing each other and another row along each wall. Pat's boots hit the ground first and he immediately filled his hand with his Winchester and led his horse to a back stall on the left side against the wall. He then started to unsaddle the sweaty horse.

Jake climbed down and walked to the two horses that caught his eye. "These are pretty fine animals," he said to Pat, then he led his young stallion to a stall on the opposite side of the stable.

Both men had their mounts unsaddled and were wiping down their sweaty horses when a shadow fell across the dirt floor. Pat could see the shadow but Jakes back was to the door. As Jake was wiping the back of his horse, everything went silent momentarily. Suddenly he heard a voice he knew wasn't Pat's.

When he looked back, he realized the stranger hadn't seen him. Dressed in black, he wasn't a little man. He was as tall as Jake and a few pounds lighter, Heavy black eyebrows and a square jaw made him quite noticeable at first sight. His short, barreled Colt with black grips, set in a shiny, short cut black, holster. The whole rig leaned back leaving the muzzle pointed a little forward, just as Joe had described. This rig suited him perfect for the line of work he was in. The holster had a white star stamped into the leather but there were no bullet loops on the belt. The man wore a gray shirt with a red cravat, and a gray, high crowned hat with a snakeskin hat band with the rattles still attached. His black pants covered his boots, all in all, he was well dressed.

The gunman locked his eyes on Pat, then he spoke. "I come to feed my horse but that'll have to wait," he said. Pat looked up to see the man that spoke. Seeing the gunman, he slowly lowered his hand to his belt. Before he could grip the gun, the stranger drew and filled the stable with smoke and thunder. When Pat saw his hand drop, he dove to the right further into the stall.

The gunman's bullet blew splinters off a post inches away from where Pat had stood. As Pat hit the ground, he filled his hand with the Colt. Just then, Jake stepped to the left and the gunman caught a glimpse of Jake's movement out of the corner of his eye and started to turn.

Faster than lightning, Jake ripped his iron out of his holster, and at fifteen feet, shot the gunman twice directly in the side of his chest blowing him backwards into a manure covered stall. With the sound of the shots, all the horses spooked and tried to get away from the thunder.

Just as they stepped onto the boardwalk, they heard a single shot, quickly followed by two more. They quickly glanced at each other and slipped into the shadows of the narrow alleyway, then walked to the edge of the Back street. They both thought that the men they hunted would be at their mercy inside the stable, but they never thought the last two shots they heard put an end to Vince Archer.

Shaken, Pat got to his feet and walked over to the man who was still trying to breathe. Slowly, he knelt down at his side and watched him take his last breath. Jake bent down and picked up the gunman's Colt lying in the dry manure. This pistol instantly captured his eye: it had been totally engraved and carved from the front sight all the way back ending at the bottom of the grips. This gun was a work of art, Jake could tell this pistol was Vince Archer's proudest possession and probably the only friend he had.

Jake first admired it and the artwork that covered this piece of steel then tucked it behind his belt. This one he would keep. Then he unbuckled the gunman's holster and handed it to Pat. "Strap this on, you're gonna be needing it I think." Pat looked at the strange holster and leaned his Winchester against a stall while he strapped the dead gunman's rig around his waist.

That was the first time since they left the army, Jake saw Pat wear a holster. "Well, he shot that plan all to hell. Everybody in town knows we're here," Pat said with a slight snicker. This guy damn near had you Pat. We got one down and two to go," Jake said.

CHAPTER

7

Jake opened the gate on his Colt, shucked out two empties and slid in two more of the big bullets then tucked it back into his holster. He pulled the gunman's pistol and again admired it momentarily then replaced the one spent shell and stuffed it back behind his belt. "We got no choice Jake, we got to go hunting and by now they know we're here." "I want to go to the hotel first, to talk to Mary. They're staying there," Jake said. Pat answered with an agreeable nod.

 The two manhunters, ready for what may come, stepped out of the stable doors into the light, the bright sun at their backs. They were both nervous and on edge they realizes this day was only going too worse. They hadn't gone far when the two gunmen they hunted stepped out of the shadows between two buildings.

When Jake saw the two men he froze in his tracks, his hand instinctively dropped to his holster. With one glance he knew who they were. They weren't dressed like cattlemen or farmers. The tools they used were strapped around their waste. The one on the left, Meeks, needed a shave pretty bad. He wore a gray silk looking vest and had his pants tucked deep into his high black polished boots. Sun reflecting off the nickel-plated Colt he wore in a front draw holster immediately caught Jake's eye. He had his hat pulled down to block the sun he now faced. Leather gauntlets on each wrist covered the cuffs of his shirt. The fact that he was a gunman was obvious to anyone who saw him.

His friend on his right, Collins, wore a brown flat crowned hat, pulled down and tied with a chin lanyard. He wore no gloves, he had leather tie downs below his elbows holding the sleeves in place on a snow-white shirt. The white shirt was accented with a narrow, black, cloth, tie. His pinstriped pants looked new with a stiff sharp crease running from his belt to his boots. This one wore a black well-worn Colt with iron wood grips like Jake's. He was clean shaven except for a black mustache that hung to his chin. The shoulder rig he wore had a black leather strap running across his chest, this he couldn't hide. Jake couldn't tell from this distance what filled that holster.

These were hard, grim, men. The type of men that lived in barrooms and brothels, the type of men that never saw a sun rise; these men never had a dollar they didn't earn with a gun. Men like these had black hearts, they breathed trouble and never saw a peaceful day in their lives. If Jake was at his best today, that would all come to an end for these men and Jake with Pat would walk away. Pat saw them about the same time and stopped dead. As instinct demanded, the two men side stepped, separating themselves by a good twelve feet.

The two gunman, walking side by side, were somewhat surprised when they saw them step out of the stable and into the light. They knew then Vince Archer was dead. There was forty five to fifty yards between them by the time they saw Jake and the Marshall. At that distance, the chances of getting off a good shot with a pistol were at best slim and everybody knew it.

When the two gunmen saw them separate,

they began to move forward, they had to close the distance and all four men knew why. Pat Winchester in his right hand and the barrel resting on his shoulder, thumbed back the hammer as he brought the rifle to bare. In a lightning-fast move, he shouldered the gun and shot the gunman in the right shoulder where it would do the most good, blowing him over backwards in the fine dust.

Unable to handle his gun, he rolled over and started to crawl, leaving a trail of blood as he tried to get out of the line of fire. At the same time, the man on the left pulled his Colt in what Jake described as faster than the blink of an eye, thumbed off two quick shots, one of which snatched at Jake's shirt, tearing a hole just above the elbow while the other buried itself in the dirt at Jake's feet.

Jake quickly moved to the right as he pulled his pistol and thumbed off a wild shot. Not seeing any reaction, he squatted low, raised his iron and took a high aim, dropping the hammer. Instantly, the last gunman standing dropped his Colt and grabbed his stomach with both hands, just as Pat drew a deadly bead on him.

"Don't shoot Pat," Jake commanded. Pat looked at Jake, "We need one of them alive," he said, then Pat relaxed his aim. As he started to lower his rifle, the gut shot gunman clumsily picked up his iron with two bloody hands out of the dry dirt and raised it to fire.

Pat, seeing his move, quickly glanced down the barrel and dropped the hammer, shooting the gut shot man, Collins directly in the head. A deadly shot at this distance was nothing for a rifleman like him. Jake always said, "you don't ever want Pat Brennon after you with a rifle." Today, he showed that statement to be true and accurate.

Jake holstered his gun and walked up to the man with the shoulder rig. For a moment, he just stood and looked; Pat's bullet had punched a small purple hole just above his left eye and created a mess on its way out.

He knelt down and unbuckled the narrow strap running across his shirt then grabbed the birds head Colt by the handle and slipped the rig off his shoulder. "You won't be needing this," he said to the man lying in the dirt and blood.

Just then Pat walked up and Jake looked up at him. "What you think you'll find when you turn out his pockets?" Pat asked. "I'll bet we find a hand full of gold eagles," Jake answered. Jake reached over and stuck his fingers in his pockets and turned them inside out.

As they thought, five gold coins fell to the dirt. Jake reached down and picked up the coins and the bloody Colt of the dead man. "We might want to go talk to this guy laying over here before he checks out," Pat said.
Just then Willard walked up, wiping sweat off his forehead with a red bandana. "These two had bad trouble writ all over 'em, I knew it the minute I seen em, Where's the third one, he looked worst of the bunch"? The old sheriff asked. "He's in the stable and he's as dead as this one," Jake said. "Willard, you think you can get Doc Jones to the jail. Me and Jake here will drag him over there, I got some questions for this guy," Pat said.

The quiet Marshall turned and headed for Main Street as Jake walked back into the stable and looked at the dead gunman lying in a pool of blood. He knelt down and turned out his pockets, again several twenty-dollar gold coins appeared.

Jake picked them up and cradled them in his hand. "Was it worth it?" he said to the dead gunslinger and walked out of the barn.

Pat took his bandana from around his neck and tied it around the fallen gunman's arm. When Jake got to him, they lifted the weak semiconscious man to his feet and drug him to the sheriff's office on the Main street.

Once inside, they dropped him down on a cot in a cell. "There ain't much left of that arm, Doc's gonna want to cut that off," Jake said. He looked down at Meeks who looked back up at him as he moaned.

"I think your gun fighting days are over," Jake said. Meeks just looked away as if he didn't hear. Jake and Pat waited for old doc Jones to get there. It wasn't but a couple minutes when Willard pushed open the door and was closely followed by the white-headed old man.

Black bag in hand, the old doctor set down on the edge of the cot in the cell and took off the bandage. He then quickly tied it back tight. "This guy is gonna die if I don't take this arm off right away and he ain't awake for me to ask," he said.

"I wanna have words with him before you

start whacking, Doc," Jake said. "I gotta do this while he's out, he ain't gonna be talking for a while Jake, so you might wanna go get a drink or some dinner cause he's out cold and he might not wake up," the old doctor said.

Jake and Pat looked at each other and left Willard standing with one bleeding gunslinger and a white-headed old doctor with a bone saw in his hand. The two left the office and headed for the hotel. They wanted to go through their rooms: they needed names and just maybe, something about where crown might be. Jake had already rounded up all the pistols, now he wanted information.

When they walked in, Mary looked at the two of them, she was happy to see Jake, she always feared someday things might not go so well. "Well, you're still alive, that's something. You're looking for room eight and nine. They haven't been touched, I knew you'd be along," she said in a happy tone and handed them the keys. As always, both men touched the rim of their hat out of respect. Pat said, "Thank you Mary." Then they climbed the stairs.

Jake took one key and Pat took the other.

When they came out Jake was carrying two Winchester rifles and two saddlebags and Pat had a rifle and a set of bags. "There wasn't anything but the usual," Jake said. Pat nodded in agreement and together they went down the stairs carrying the dead man's belongings. Jake walked up to Mary and politely asked.

"The rooms been paid for Mary?" Mary shook her head and softly said, "No they owe twelve dollars but I'll settle for one of those rifles." Jake looked at the two rifles, after a short moment, he handed her one over the counter. "It's the best of the two," he said, then he reached in his pocket and produced a double eagle and dropped it on the counter.

"Jake, you don't have to pay their due," she said. Jake politely nodded and replied, "This is from Vince, he's covering both rooms." Mary got a slight smile and raked the coin off the counter.

It was late afternoon when the two walked into the café and dropped down at their usual table. Without a word, the waitress brought a small pot of coffee and two cups and set them between the two men. "You think you could fry us up a couple steaks with a couple boiled potatoes?" Pat asked. The waitress smiled big and answered, "Coming up Marshall."

"When we get done here Pat, I wanna go see if our one-armed friend can tell us anything," Jake said. Pat nodded and the two men sat in silence. Tired, but no longer hungry, they paid for their dinner and headed for Willard's office. When they stepped through the door, Doc Jones was buttoning up his coat and just leaving. "There's an angel on this fella's shoulder, he should be dead, but he's awake and full of laudanum, so he might tell you anything you wanna know.

When Jake looked in, the cell door was standing wide open, Willard was stuffing his Colt in his holster and putting on his hat. "Pat, you killed these bastards and you aughta be the one paying for them to be planted," Willard said. Pat smiled and flipped the sheriff a gold eagle he had taken off Collins on back street. "This should cover it," Pat said, then he grabbed a chair and walked into the cell with the one-armed gunman.

Lying motionless and flat on his back, Meeks moaned in pain as he turned his head and looked up at Pat. Slurring his words while slobber ran out of the corner of his mouth, Pat could barely understand what he said. "You're the one that shot me, ain't ya?" "Yeah, and you're lucky, I could have taken your head off, like your friend Collins." Pat said as he dropped down in the chair.

"Now, you listen real good. You remember seeing that pen when you rolled into town?" Meeks slowly blinked his eyes and tried to nod his head. Pat knew he heard and understood. "You throwed down and took a shot at a US Marshall. In thirty days I can have you in that dirty pen you passed back there for five years. But if you give me answers, you can ride out of Las Animas as soon as you are able."

Meeks never moved, he just stared at Pat. Pat knew he was too weak to talk. "I'll be back in the morning; you talk to me then or you'll be on the short track to that gray bar hotel. Meeks looked away; he knew exactly what Pat meant. Pat stepped out of the cell and locked the door, Meeks watched him turn the key and looked back at the wall. It was late afternoon and neither man wanted to start the fifteen-mile ride back to the ranch so once again they walked into the little café that was but a couple hundred yards from the sheriff's office where the last of the hired gunmen lay.

After a quick dinner they walked into the saloon. The other drinkers, most of whom Jake had grown up with and Pat had come to know, greeted them with a friendly nod or a pleasant hello. Someone at the bar they didn't see told the bartender, "Drink 'em on me." Jake pulled up a chair at a corner table as usual.

It wasn't long when the apron clad bartender walked up and set a bottle of rye and two glasses in the center of the table then turned and without a word and walked away. While they drank the harsh whiskey, they sat discussing the problem they had, Forest Crown. What was he doing in La junta, just nineteen miles from where they now Sat, and how would they find and deal with him?"

The one solid answer they came up with, was they would never feel safe with him alive. Early the next morning, Jake and Pat met over a cup of coffee in the same chairs they sat in the day before. "I'm going over to that jail, and Meeks will tell me what I want to know or I'll put my boot on that bloody stump of his," Jake said. Pat grinned; he knew Jake was serious.

When they walked into the sheriff's office, Willard was standing over the wood stove pouring a cup of coffee. "Is he still alive, Willard?" Pat asked. "Yeah, and I told him there's a half dozen men just like him in that pen that you put there and if he ain't careful, he'd be the next. I got the feeling he'll tell you what you want," Willard said as he yawned.

Pat walked up and looked between the bars. Meeks was just sitting up on the edge of his bunk and was shaking like a man in ice water. A blood-soaked bandage was tied to what was left of his right arm. He didn't try to talk he looked a pale gray color, Jake thought he looked dead. "You got a smoke Marshall?" he asked in a weak voice. Jake was surprised when he spoke, he didn't think Meeks would be alive this morning.

Pat looked around and glanced at Willard. "Naw, I don't smoke, but Willard here will roll you one," Pat answered as he unlocked the cell door. Hearing this, Willard pulled out a little white bag and started twisting up a smoke for Meeks.

"You know Marshall, I've killed at least thirty men, most of them during the war. My folks had a right nice farm back in Carolina, I was fifteen at the time. Then one day Sherman with that army of his rode in and burnt everything he saw to the ground so I had very little choice. I rode west and this is how it turned out. You know Marshal, life can be a full of surprises. Now I'm gonna wind up back there, swatting mosquitos with one arm," Meeks said.

Willard handed Pat the small cigarette and a stick match with a blue head. Meeks reached out and took the home rolled and match and looked at Jake. "The first thing I have to learn is how to light this," then he cracked a subtle grin on his dry lips.

"Whatta you wanna know Marshall?" He asked. "We need to know about Crown," Jake snapped. Meeks popped the match with his thumbnail and set fire to the still wet cigarette.

As he exhaled the white smoke he said, "He sold seven-hundred head of cattle and bought a spread in La Junta, at least, that's what he told me. Then he moved all his horses out here. He found out by accident you two were in Bent County and he can't live with that, he's gonna kill both of ya. He put two thousand gold on each of ya," he said as smoke drifted into the air.

"Now I ain't seen the spread, but from what he says, he's pretty well set up. Collins told me he has a half dozen riders there at the ranch. I don't know if they're gun hands or ranch hands, but they're there," he said as he blew out more white smoke.

"Marshall, I want to know why you didn't kill me when you were shooting?" Meeks asked. Pat hesitated for a moment. "I was gonna but Jake here stopped me. He said he needed answers." Meeks looked up at Jake. "Well, I guess I'm alive thanks to you," he said. "Yeah, you're alive and you can ride out of here. Your friends have a face full of dirt about now, so you came out better than them," Jake said. Meeks agreed with a slight nod.

Just as Pat opened the door to leave, Meeks spoke again. "Oh yeah Marshall, one more thing. I rode in on the train with a fella named Luke Latrell, he rides with a Mexican. You'll know the Mex when you see him, he has a gold tooth. I think you might have heard of Latrell," he said, then his gaze returned to the floor.

Hearing the name Luke Latrell Pat's head snapped around. Jake was somewhat surprised to see the expression on Pat's face turn ice cold as he looked at the one-armed gunman and then headed for the boardwalk. Jake pulled the door closed behind them and Pat stopped in his tracks. Jake wasn't going to ask; he knew Pat was fixing to let him know.

"I've been holding paper on Latrell for over a year. He's wanted in Arizona, Utah, the New Mexico territory and in Nevada and California. He leaves bodies everywhere he goes. They don't get no worse than him Jake. He'll face ya straight up or shoot you in the back, he doesn't care. This guy killed his own father when he was fifteen-years old and he's been stacking 'em up ever since. From what I've been told, he's as fast as they come.

You put 'em all together and there's at least five thousand on him. I don't know about the Mex. I ain't fooling with Latrell, Jake. I'll shoot him on sight," Pat said.

CHAPTER

8

"Let's talk to Willard, Pat. I wanna find out who the law is in La Junta and what he knows about him. Maybe he can be of help when we get there," Jake said. Pat knew they would wind up in La Junta, it just hadn't been said yet. Now it was in the open and Pat was ready to ride.

Jake turned and stuck his head in the office door. "Willard, let's go get some coffee," Jake said. Willard came from around the desk and put on his hat. " I know you boys want something, but I sure don't need any more coffee. What can I do for you?" Willard asked? Instead of the café, they found themselves at the saloon. Willard immediately grabbed himself a glass of warm beer before he sat down with the two.

"Tell us about the Sheriff over in La Junta."

Pat said. Willard sipped the beer and took his hat off. "Ted Nelson been a friend of mine more than ten years. He seldom leaves town, he'll help you if he can. You met him before Pat," Willard said. "Yeah, I met him. I know he totes a shotgun, I just don't know much about the guy," Pat said.

"He's straight up Pat. The best thing you can do is let him know what's going on," he said as he leaned back in his chair and sipped his beer.

"We can be in La, Junta in a few hours if we leave now," Jake said. Without another word the two men headed directly for the livery stable. It was less than a day's ride to the little town and they had business to handle there.   It was midafternoon when they rode into La, Junta. Over the years, both men had been there numerous times for one reason or another. When Jake was still in school, he cut class on more than one occasion and rode to La Junta to visit Pearl's Palace with several other boys his age.

Pearls was a high end, well known brothel. It sat two stories tall, with four white pillars in between the windows, making it look somewhat like a mansion on the end of town. It was whitewashed from top to bottom the cut glass panels in the front double doors let a red glow filter through the glass. Like all brothels, it had bright red silky curtains hanging from ceiling to floor and red fuzzy wallpaper.

The Palace had a separate room with three copper bathtubs. Pipes coming out of the bottom of the tubs stuck through the wall to drain off the water. Many cowhands coming off the range paid that extra dollar to have their back washed by the lady of their choice. Jake, like many boys his age, found their first thrill with a lady at Pearl's.

Pearls sat on the far west end of the town separate from the rest of the businesses. That's what it took to keep the peace amongst the ladies and the church going folk that lived in the little town, even though it was rumored the preacher had been seen coming and going through the back door.

"You ever been to Pearl's?" Pat asked as they rode. Jake grinned a little. "I was about fourteen the first time I went there, I give them ladies the first five-dollar gold I ever had. It took me a month to earn that gold. I got home from school late that night, my pa met me before I got into the house. He laughed a little and told me I smelled like them ladies and he didn't want my mom to smell that perfume all over me, so I bathed in the trough under the windmill. That was the best five dollars I ever spent," Jake replied. Pat broke into full laughter.

It was late afternoon, and the two men were tired and sweaty when they got first sight of the east end of town. The train tracks run east and west then curved north for a short piece then again turned west running along the edge of the little town. La, Junta was nothing new for the two men, they knew the road like the road to their own houses. Jake reined the young, black stallion to the shade of an old cottonwood and climbed out of the saddle. While he was trying to stretch the kinks out of his back, Pat was pouring water in his hat for his thirsty horse.

"I wanna lay back a while Pat, till the sun is low. I would like to ride in without being seen. Chances are, Crown knows by now his men are dead and for all we know someone could be waiting for us," Jake said. When the sweaty horse raised her muzzle out of his hat, Pat put it back on. As the cool water dripped down his back, he took his badge and slipped it into his pocket.

Killing time made Jake nervous and so he paced and watch the western horizon. When the sun was little more than half below the skyline Jake checked his cinch and swung into the saddle, Pat following. With a slight nudge, Pat's mare moved in front of the black. He hesitated for a minute before they crossed the tracks.

Once they crossed, Jake began to look around as they rode, looking for anything that looked odd or different. Bold as brass, Pat led him up the middle of the main street where they tied up at the sheriff's office. Before he climbed out of the saddle, Jake flipped the tie on his Colt. Pat looking around slowly, climbed down with his Winchester in hand.

The sun was well below the mountains now and the kerosene lanterns sent their yellow glow across the boardwalks and into the dusty streets, the dim light reflected off the glass windows and the dark overtook everything.   As they lashed their mounts to the hitching post, they heard the tinny ring of a piano telling them the saloon was open for business. The saloon was the last thing on their minds, now all they thought of was Forest Crown and where to find him. They knew when they found Crown, they would find Luke Latrell.

Still on the alert, they stepped into the sheriff's office to find it empty. Pat took off his hat and peered around the small room. Jake looked around a short minute then sat on the corner of the desk. "You want to get something to eat, Jake?" Pat asked. Pat glanced out the window to see the well-lit board walk in front of the corner café.

Jake pushed his hat back on his head and thought a minute. "Yeah, I could go for dinner, if I remember right, they have pretty good food there." "Anything is better than what we've been eating the last couple days," Pat said with a laugh. Jake smiled.

Pat unconsciously reached up to make sure his badge was out of sight then stepped through the office door. Jake dropped his hand to his Colt to find it unlashed, then they started across the dark street. The little café was on the other side of the street and down three doors. It stood alone with a narrow alley on each side of the building, this in itself was a reason for caution.

The two men walked and searched, their

eyes on the constant hunt for the men who hunted them. As they walked, the only sound was that of their boots and the ring of their spurs on the boardwalk. In the distance they could hear the faint ring of the piano in the saloon.

When they got to the café, Jake turned the knob and pushed the door open. Before he walked in, his eyes immediately searched the room. Red and white checkered cloths covered a half dozen square tables that were placed around the little room.

The place was empty except for a tall dark-headed waitress who was placing silverware on a table near the front door. In the corner, with his back to the wall, Ted Nelson sat with a fork in his hand chewing on a piece of tuff meat. The first thing Jake saw was the shiny badge pinned to his plaid wool shirt; his short, barreled shotgun was leaned against the wall within arm's reach. Jake knew who Ted Nelson was, but until now he never paid any attention to the man himself.

Now Jake saw him as a big, burly, gruff man that never smiled and if he wanted, could pull your arms off like the wings of a moth. Jake saw this man with his gun as a man that didn't take any chances.

When Ted saw Pat, he motioned with his head to come over. Pat smiled and walked to his table, his spurs ringing as he walked across the wood floor. Jake, a couple feet behind, followed. Pat leaned his rifle against the wall next to Ted's shotgun, then pulled out a chair and sat down. Jake slid a chair from an empty table and set across from the window, which he didn't particularly like. "I been expecting you Pat," Ted said. "Ted, this is Jake Cleary," Pat said. "I know Jake, I've seen him around here for years, it's pretty hard not to know who he is," he said with a smile.

"I heard about the killing in Las Animas, they didn't have dirt in their faces before I heard about it" Ted said. "You know how gossip travels, Pat," he added. "We're gonna get a bite to eat, then we need to go to your office and have a talk," Pat said. Jake sat silent.

In less than an hour Jake pushed open the sheriff's door. Ted was sitting at his desk; he had a long black smoking cigar clinched between his teeth. On his desk sat a checkerboard with the pieces lined up. Pat stepped in and took off his hat, dropping down in a chair. Jake walked over and leaned against the wall and listened to Pat tell him the whole story from start to finish.

"I'll do anything I can to help you boys. I knew he was no good when he rolled into town with all those gunmen walking in his shadow." Ted said. "Ted, you know, we can't ride out to his ranch, we might as well shoot ourselves we ride out there," Pat said. "Does Crown ever come into town"? Jake asked.

Ted got a big smile on his face. "You know there's the prettiest gal you ever saw that works at Pearl's. Hearing this, Jake began to wonder what the hell that had to do with the simple question.   She's a big, busty gal, gotta be near six feet tall with honey colored hair and the bluest eyes, she's really something. He comes in with a couple of his gunmen every couple days to see her, he always rides in before sundown. He chases her like he's a hound and she's a bitch in heat." Jake got a smile, he now understood.

"When he comes, they tie up around back, and then his men look around inside before he goes in, then he leaves them on the front porch with a bottle until he comes out. He usually stays all night, I guess he don't like riding at night. They really love him at Pearl's, I guess he drops a few yellow coins when he leaves," Ted said.

Jake looked up. "He leaves how many men on the front porch?" he asked. "Usually, two. They'll sit on that porch and sip that whiskey and puff cigars all night until he walks out," Ted answered with a grin. Hearing this Jake and Pat had a fairly good idea how this was going to play out.

"Where is this ranch he bought? "Jake asked "About an hour and a half west of town. The road forks to the left, and a couple miles down that road is the entrance to the ranch. You'll see a stone pillar on each side of the road, that lets you know you are on the Crown property. That's as far as I went," Ted said.

"He bought the old Nichols place, it's at least three sections, the nicest spread around here," Ted added. "So, when he rides in, he'll be coming from the west," Pat asked. "Yep," Ted answered.

"You have any idea when he's due back in?" Pat asked. "He was herer night before last, cause I remember going over there and telling them girls, don't be coming out on that porch bare assed anymore," Ted answered, and chuckled a little. "So, he'll be back in, in the next couple days or so, I'd bet on it," he said.

"Now Pat, me telling you this doesn't mean its ok to shoot up my town. You figure something out because men come from all over the state to visit Pearls. The governor was even here two years ago, and I don't want no killing going on in there. Them ladies bring a lot of money to this town. If you can get 'em out of Pearls, I don't care if you drag 'em to death, but no shooting in Pearls," Ted said.

The two men looked at each other, Jake grinned slightly, and Pat nodded in agreement "Jake, you go get us some rooms and I'll take care of the horses," Pat said. Jake put his hat on and headed for the Arrowhead hotel, like Pat he was tired and wanted to flop down but he didn't like the idea of Pat walking around town alone so he stepped up the pace and quickly locked up two rooms on the west side of the of the hotel.

The sun was well below the horizon and it was darker than a bad dream. Jake stepped off the porch and looked around a little then set a fast pace for the livery stable: he didn't want Pat to get caught alone. Jake unlashed his Colt then stepped between two buildings and followed his nose to the livery stable where he found Pat.

He'd had the horses unsaddled and was dipping grain out of a sack with by the dim light of an oil lamp. "I want to ride out to the ranch in the morning," Pat said. Jake quickly glanced up at him. Before he could say anything, Pat added. "I wanna try to see how many guns he has out there." Jake knew riding out to the ranch could be a fatal mistake but he understood what Pat had in mind.

Once the horses were fed and stabled, the two tired men headed for the hotel to get some overdue sleep. The sun had just begun to show when Jake's feet hit the floor. All he had on his mind was a plate of ham and eggs and a pot of coffee. Hearing the noise in the next room, Pat threw back his blanket and glanced out the window into the gray of early morning.

Jake was the first to step into the hall and start down the stairs. Pat was less than a minute behind him. When Pat stepped onto the boardwalk, he saw Jake walk into the café across the street. The early morning was quiet, very few people were on the street at this hour, a cool breeze passed over him letting him know fall was near. They sat and drank coffee and ate a half dozen eggs. When they finished, they washed it all down with more hot coffee. They both knew they would be in the saddle in less than an hour and a half.

They had a big problem and they wanted to put an end to it. They both knew the problem of Forest Crown would only be at rest when he was underground.

CHAPTER

9

The sun was warm on their backs when they rode west out of town on a cool Colorado morning. They were looking for the Crown ranch, they knew Crown was there, now they needed to know how many gunmen he had with him. Cautiously, they moved down the westward road as Ted directed. Before they got to the turn off, the sage began to thin a little and give way to grass that made this part of Colorado perfect for the ranchers and farmers.

The abundance of surface water kept the grass, and cottonwoods and the elms green right up to the first frost. The grass fed not only cattle and horses, but large herds of deer and elk and antelope. The two men rode in silence admiring this part of the state. Straight ahead, the road began to rise a little and the trees began to thicken, reminding them they were in the mountains.

Just as Ted had said, they came to the fork in the road. From there, scattered cedars spotted the grassy fields. Off to the right, a narrow creek hidden by the willows ran alongside the road. After a while, they could see the road curve out of sight around a small tree covered hill on their left. When they could no longer see down the road, Jake loosened his pistol in his holster. Pat pulled his rifle from the scabbard and laid it across his lap.

Jake riding at Pat's left side, spurred the young stallion up the hill and over the top with Pat close behind into the small trees. It didn't take long for the young, strong stallion to reach the crest of the hill. Once at the top Jake cautiously weaved his way forward between the thicket of trees with Pat moving in behind him. Jake turned in the saddle and said, "I wasn't riding around that blind curve, I ain't in the mood for any surprises, if you know what I mean." he said.

From atop his horse, Jake saw something through an opening in the trees and quickly reined in. Pat laid back on his reins and at the same time they slid out of the saddle. Pat had his reins in one hand and his Winchester in the other.

Casually, Jake walked the young horse to the edge of the clearing, keeping in the shadows as much as possible. Pat moved to his side, just as Jake tied his reins to the bough of a small pine. Jake looked over at Pat who was tying up his horse. Down the slope and at a little over six-hundred yards, sat exactly what they were looking for. "Let's see that spy glass of yours Pat," Jake said.

Pat reached in his bags and grabbed the glass as Jake sat down and leaned against a stump. Jake propped the glass on his knees to steady his view. Pat looked around in all directions making sure they were alone while Jake peered through the scope.

"You wanna take a look at this Pat?" I count three of 'em, two on the porch and one more by the corral," Jake said as he handed Pat the glass. Pat sat down next to Jake and pressed the telescope to his right eye and searched.

In a low, muffled tone, Jake could hear him counting. One, two, and three. I can only see three that look like gun hands Jake, the one at the corral and the two on the porch. The one at the corral wears a front draw rig," Pat said. Then he went on. "There's three or four more down there but they look like hands. If I'm right, Latrell is down there, and he wears a front draw rig according to the fliers I got," Pat said.

In a way Jake liked hearing this. He knew there was big money on the man with the front draw rig. They looked at each other for a second then mounted up and started back in their own tracks. Soon, they came out of the small trees and Jake reined in and looked down on the creek and the road that brought them there.

From this high point he could see for miles. The grass was a bright green, along the edges of the stream it spread out in spots making little patches of emerald, an occasional willow bent to the demands of the light breeze that just came up.

Jake was just about to touch his mount with his spurs when he saw a trail of dust nearly a mile off floating above the road. "Look Pat," he said as he pointed toward the dust. Both men reined around and went back in the cover of the small trees.

There they sat watching the puff of dust get closer. As soon as they could see a horse in front of the dust, Pat reached back and pulled out the brass telescope, stretching it out full then putting it to his eye. Jake sat and watched the horse coming closer at a slow trot.

The horse was now roughly four hundred yards out when Jake heard Pat say in a low tone. "Well hello Mister Boone, I knew you looked familiar, now you're wearing a gun." Jake had no idea who Mister Boone was, but Pat knew him and that meant something. When Boone was no more than three hundred yards from the base of the hill, Pat said, "Come on Jake, there's an old friend I need to talk to," then he set his spurs. With Jake close at his side the two rode off the hill in a cloud of red dust.

Before Boone knew what was happening, Pat quickly reined up at his left side. Jake pulled up in front of the startled horse and stopped dead. "Jake I'd like you to meet Mr. Levi Boone. He's the new hostler in Las Animas, aren't you Levi?"

Before he could say anything, Pat pulled his boot out of the stirrup and kicked him out of his saddle where he lay on his back in the red dust. His horse being surrounded by two other horses, flinched, and bucked but settled down quickly. Jake looked at Pat and could see he was really pissed.

Not knowing why Pat nailed him, Jake sprung out of the saddle and pulled the pistol from the man lying in the dirt. As Levi clumsily got to his feet, Pat said, "Get on that horse, you're going back to town. You try running and I'll shoot ya." Levi looked at Pat and saw a man that was seething. "Now you know how word travels so fast Jake, remember that gossip Ted mentioned." This guy works for Crown, he's how Crown knows his men are dead, he was in Las Animas snooping. I'm betting Crown don't know we're in town yet Jake," Pat said.

Levi got to his feet and started brushing the dust off his clothes. He then climbed into the saddle. "I ain't broke no laws, Marshall," he said. "You're involved in a plot to kill a US Marshall. You may not go to the pen for that but between me or Jake here, you'll get the worst beating you ever had, that I'm damn sure of," Pat replied.

Levi pulled his horse around in front of Pat.

"Does old man Crown know we're in town?" Jake asked. Levi didn't answer,r he just looked down at his own print in the dirt. "If I have to climb down off this horse again, I'm gonna start by breaking your ribs and end up breaking your arm, so if you're smart, you'll answer me before you hit the ground again," Jake said.

The man in the dusty shirt slowly raised his head and looked at Jake. "I don't think so, if he does, I didn't tell him," he answered. "Now, you move that horse of yours. You're going back to town and like I said, you try to run, I won't chase you, I'll shoot ya out of the saddle ," Pat snapped.

They rode a little ways and Jake turned and looked at Levi "Is there a gun at the ranch named Luke Latrell?" Jake asked. Levi looked up from his downward stare, "There is a Luke there but I don't know his last name and I ain't asking," he answered. "What kind of rig does he wear?" Pat asked. "He wears a front draw. I don't know much about him, like everyone else I stays clear of 'em." Levi answered.

"Where do the gun hands sleep?" Pat asked. They all sleep in the bunk house all but Wallace. "Who's Wallace," Pat asked. He's Mr.

Crown's personal body Gard, he sleeps in the house. Luke sleeps at the far end of the bunk house with a pistol under his blankets," Levi added. "What does he ride?" Jake asked? Levi hesitated a minute. "He rides a tall buck skin," he replied.

Pat touched his mount with his spurs and the pace quickened. In less than an hour, they saw the white pillars at Pearls palace shining in the midday sun. Jake looked over at their prisoner, "You ain't got far to go, you'll be indoors for the next few days," he said. Levi raised his stare and looked around a little as though looking for help.

When they walked in the office, Ted was putting papers in the small safe that sat in the corner under the rifle rack. Like all western towns, a safe in a sheriff's office was as common as jail bars.

"I'm gonna lock him up here for a few days Ted, I don't want him carrying tales to Crown," Pat said. "I never give him any thought, he worked out at the old Nichols spread, he must have stayed on after Crown bought the place," Ted said as he walked up and looked at Levi, who was gazing at the cell Pat was unlocking. "You know Levi, you're lucky he didn't bust you up," he said as he gestured to Jake with his thumb. Levi stood silent and stared at the floor.   Without a word, he walked into the cell and dropped his hat on the bunk as Pat locked the door. "I'm due for some lunch, you boys care for a bite?" Ted asked. The two agreed with a nod and the three men walked out of the office and headed straight for the café. Pat glanced down making sure once more his badge was out of sight., Jake felt his holster making sure his Colt was lashed down.

Now all they could do was wait. The two had worked up a plan of sorts to get Crown when he visited Pearls, but the part of waiting was the part neither man did well. The men never spoke of it but they knew Crown would not stop.   He had created conditions where Jake and Pat had to take their women out of town because of his over whelming hunger for vengeance. That alone they would not forgive.

On the second day, Pat brought Levi his meal just as he had done the morning and evening before. He noticed his prisoner was getting a little antsy and was beginning to pace the cell. Pat was getting tired of the wait. They had Ted watching

145

the west road into town and they too kept an eye on Pearls.

It was midafternoon on the third day and there wasn't a cloud in the sky; the sun had given up its stranglehold on summer and there was a cool breeze on Jake's back. On that day when Jake stepped out of the shadows into the bright sun, he saw three horsemen a half mile off riding three abreast coming into town.

Seeing the men and horses, he stepped onto the boardwalk and into the shade. For a second, he looked around: on the other side of the road, he saw Pat coming up the boardwalk with his Winchester in hand. When Pat saw Jake he turned and started across the road, Jake knew then he hadn't seen the oncoming riders.

"You know Jake, this is getting old," Pat said. Before he said anymore, Jake motioned with his thumb in the direction of the riders. On the boardwalk now, Pat turned to see the reason for the three day wait. Just as Ted had said, when they got to Pearl's, they rode to the back as though they didn't want to be seen.

"I can't tell from here if Latrell is one of 'em," Pat said. "If Ted is right, we'll be seeing Mr.

Crown in the morning," Pat said. Just then, Jake saw Ted coming down the boards heading in their direction, he was keeping a steady pace. "You boys see the three horses ride in?" Ted asked. "Yeah, we seen 'em," Pat said. "Didn't you tell us he spends the night there when he comes?" Jake asked. Ted answered with a nod.

"You wouldn't know if he's an early riser, would ya?" Jake asked. "He'll get up and go over to the café with his men and have breakfast before he leaves town, I've seen him do it twice. When he's here, I keep an eye on him and his men," Ted answered.

Jake looked at Pat and smiled and Pat grinned at the sheriff. They found out what they needed to know, now all they had to do was wait for sunup.

They walked over to the saloon and grabbed a table in the corner where they sat and slowly sipped a bottle of rye while they hatched of the simple plan to get Crown. Under the veil of night, they walked to the café and finished the day with roast beef, and boiled potatoes and coffee as usual.

"It ain't home cooking but it will damn sure

do," Jake said. Pat dropped some coins on the table and cautiously looked around before they stepped onto the street. Pat flipped open his silver watch and quickly snapped it closed. "One of these days I'll get me one of those," Jake said, as he glanced at Pat's watch.

Jake had no idea what time it was when he was awakened by Pat thumping on the wall. He glanced out the window and saw it was just as black as when he walked into the hotel. The two men had to get saddled and be down the road before the lights came on at Pearls. There would be no breakfast this morning for the two, today they were going to put an end to a problem that had come out of nowhere and totally upset their lives. They met in the hall at just about the same time, both men were wearing pistols and carrying rifles. Pat was wearing the rig of the gun fighter Jake killed in Las Animas two weeks before. Not saying a word, they walked down the stairs and into the street. Once they reached barber shop, they cut a short trail to the livery.

By the dim light of an oil lamp, they saddled and made ready for their early morning ride. Side by side, they rode out of the stable. The familiar lights of town had yet to be lit, leaving the little town as dark as the night. The only light they saw were the stars in the sky reflecting off the water in the troughs as they rode by. There was a slight breeze that told them summer was gone and to expect fall. Their horses were well rested and moved as though they liked the freedom from the stable.

In the dark they were at somewhat of a disadvantage, they needed a certain amount of light to find the exact place from where they would make their play. They had been in the saddle about an hour when Jake reached back and pulled a cloth sack from his bags, producing several stiff strips of beef, he had brought from Las Animas. In the dark, he reached over and handed a couple strips of the dried beef to Pat. Pat stuck one between his teeth and the other he slipped in his shirt pocket. "You wouldn't have a cup of coffee in there would you Jake? "he asked with a laugh. Somewhere in the distance they heard the faint bawl of a calf, soon followed by the howl of a coyote. Both men were a little on edge: this was the morning they were going to put an end to the problem that had dogged them and totally disrupted their lives for the last several weeks.

Jake reined in and turned his mount around facing east. "I think we're close Pat," he said. Pat turned and leaned on his saddle horn, watching as the fast-moving light of early morning came their way.

Soon there would be three riders coming down the road they now occupied, two of which were professional gun hands. While they watched and waited, the morning sun peeked over the horizon making the morning dew sparkled like diamonds on the green grass. Now they could see the road they just passed over. Until now, they had never noticed this narrow road was cut into the side of a hill.

From the position they now held, they saw the left side of the road quickly rose while the right side quickly dropped down and leveled off at the bottom. Both sides of the road were pretty well covered by grass. Jake looked down to the stream and saw a cow elk and several deer peacefully grazing on the lush grasses.

At the bottom, a small stream weaved its way through the tall grass, Jake figured it was the lower end of the stream that ran alongside the road. Jake had lived in Bent county all his life. He'd rode in every corner of Colorado and passed through La Junta dozens of times and until now, he'd never seen this area with all the rich grasses.

Now he knew why Crown had bought a ranch here. He reined right and took his horse down to the water. Pat followed, and they let their horses graze on the dew-covered grass.

Pat flipped open the face of his watch. "Jake, the way I figure it, those boys will be along shortly." Jake heard Pat and they moved a little farther down the road. There they found the place where they could stay out of sight and still have a clear view of the road they now traveled.

Jake sat and chewed on the dried meat while Pat peered through the scope searching the hills. Out of habit, Jake spun the cylinder on his Colt.

CHAPTER

10

It was nearing eight o:clock when Jake first saw the three riders walking their horses down the dirt road. This road was little more than a wagon trail beat into the ground by generations of men and their horses and wagons for one reason or another. Out of habit, Jake reached down and loosened his gun in his holster. Pat pulled his Colt and rested it on his leg then lifted his Winchester and set it back to rest.

When the three riders came within thirty yards, Jake spurred the young black and quickly stopped him in the middle of the road. Pat, six feet to Jake's right sat, staring at the men who had been hunting them.

They guessed Crown to be the one in the gray and white shirt. On each side and back a horses length sat the two gunmen that occupied the porch of the brothel the night before.

Seeing Jake and Pat, they reined their horses forward, putting Crown in the rear as to protect him. Jake noticed Crown had a leather strap running across his white shirt, tying down the pistol he wore under his coat

Before their horses came to a complete stop the gunman on Pat's side drew his pistol, and in a split second sent a hot slug directly towards Pat. With the roar of the first shot all the horses spooked and reared up but not before the first bullet cut a deep groove in the top of Pat's right leg just above the knee.   In the blink of an eye, the gunman on Jake's side drew and fired, his shot going wild. Instantly, Jake, drew his Colt and returned fire just before his startled young horse threw him to the ground. Jake hit the ground with his Colt in his right hand and his reins in his left.

Still on the ground and trying to control a frightened horse that was tugging on the reins, Jake re cocked and sent off another shot towards the rider on his side. For a second, he thought he might have wounded the gunman, then the hired gunman spurred his horse and headed up the hill.

By now, Pat had his horse somewhat under control and returned fire. With this shot, the rider on his side spurred his horse to Pat's right and headed down toward the creek then seeing he was blocked by a wall of willows turned his mount back the way they came.

"You alright Pat?" Jake hollered. "Yeah, I'm ok. Go run him down," Pat answered. Jake, his Colt still in hand, sprung into the saddle and clipped the black with his heels, heading for the uphill rider. By the time Jake was in the clear, he saw the gunman go over the top of the rise.

Pat, with blood running down his leg, holstered his pistol. In an attempt to stop the bleeding, he pushed his gloved hand down hard on the six-inch gash, the pain was vicious. Seeing it wasn't a deadly wound, he clipped his mount and moved into the tracks of the gunman that shot him. The gunman, now heading back towards town, had over a hundred yards on him.

Jake, now at the top of the rise, reined in. Suddenly, he felt the wind from a bullet whiz past his head, then heard the crack of a rifle. Instantly, he dipped low in the saddle. Out of the corner of his eye, he saw the riderless horse standing, his reins hanging to the ground.

Jake quickly holstered his Colt and ran the black horse behind a small cedar then jumped out of the saddle while he ripped his rifle out of the scabbard. *You want a rifle fight you got one,* he thought as his boots hit the ground.

Quickly, he double tied the black horse to the cedar and started his hunt. *He'll go for his mount,* he thought, so he squatted low and headed to where he last saw the horse.

At the same time, Pat's gray was moving in behind the light brown horse. Suddenly, the gunman reined in and jumped out of the saddle in a cloud of dust. Surprised by what he did, Pat pulled right and laid back on the reins, bringing the stampeding horse to a skidding stop in a cloud of red dirt. Before the gray settled down, Pat was on his feet with his deadly rifle in hand.

While Pat looked for cover out of the open, Jake moved a few yards and stopped and listened for anything: the click of a gun, a breaking twig, anything that would tell him where the rifleman waited.

Cautiously he moved, being careful not to break that twig that might get him killed. The cedars weren't really close together, here the tops of the brush was low, so Jake had a good clear view between the trees.

It was quiet, the only sound was Pat's rifle fire in the distance, this made Jake even more nervous, so he listened. To Jake, it was too quiet, so he dropped down on his belly in the dirt and searched. Just then, he heard far off in the distance another crack of a rifle, quickly followed by another. While he laid on his belly in the dirt, he looked for the legs of the standing horse.

Pat dropped his reins and took up a position behind some thick brush. There wasn't a rock or a log anywhere, all he had was the brush to hide himself and it wasn't bullet proof. His leg had begun to throb, his pants were drenched with blood to the toe of his boots and a vicious pain was setting in. *I ain't got time to fool around with this guy,* he thought.

Just then, he heard the crack of a rifle and twigs and leaves exploded in his face. Momentarily blinded by the flying bush, he wiped his eyes with his gloved hand. He now knew the gunman had his range. Squatting low, he dodged to another bush and peered between the thick leaves.

Back and forth he scanned for any movement as he also searched for better cover. Suddenly, the lone rifleman made a fatal mistake: he started a run for his horse.

At the same time nearly a mile away Jake was still lying in the dirt when he saw something move that might put an end this fight and probably save his life. Less than fifty yards away, he saw a pair of boots and part of a leg below the branches of a cedar. Slowly, he adjusted his position to put himself clear of all the branches. Still on his belly in the dirt, he shouldered the rifle and drew a tight bead just above the top of the black boot.

Once he was sure he was on target, he dropped the hammer. The forty-four-caliber slug grazed the top of the boot and took off a piece of the leather before the slug blew out the back of the gunman's leg. Instantly, the gunman dropped his rifle and fell to the ground, then rolled on his side and started to reached down for his leg. Seeing him lying on his side, Jake took a deadly aim and shot him directly in the chest. Confident of his shot, Jake got to his feet and walked to the bloody mess lying at the base of a small tree. He had been right, he saw where his first shot grazed his shoulder, leaving a circle of blood on his shirt.

While Jake was looking at the fallen gunman, Pat stood up and quickly threw his Winchester to his shoulder, shooting the running gunman at seventy-five yards. The wounded gunman dropped to his knees and before he could regain his footing, Pat shot him again.

Jake didn't have time to check the dead gunman or his saddlebags for papers, his concern now was Pat, he knew he'd taken a bullet and now he had to get to his friend. As fast as he could run, he made it back to his waiting horse. Before he jumped in the saddle, he noticed a short red streak about three inches long and a small amount of blood high on the horses left hip. Tenderly, he reached over and rubbed the young horse near the small wound, causing him to snort and side-step. He knew then the gunman's first shot had slid along the horse's hip.

"This is why you jumped when the shooting started," he mumbled to the horse. Once atop, he started back for Pat when he saw the riderless horse standing watching him. Jake reined left and rode the fifty yards, grabbing the horse by the reins. He then headed back where he last saw Pat.

Across a little flat ground and back to the edge of the hill, Jake with an extra horse in tow followed his own tracks down the slope to the road where the shooting had started. *With all the shooting and dodging the bullets, Crown must have slipped away, unless Pat had him,* Jake thought as he rode down the side of the rise. Once to the road, Jake reined in and looked around. From here, he could see the tracks trampled through the tall grass knowing they would lead him to Pat.

Jake reached over and tied the reins of the extra to a pine bough and set off into the tracks he hoped were Pat's. He followed the trail out of the grass into the soft dirt. After a few minutes walking in the tracks, he looked up and saw, at more than a hundred yards, Pat riding the gray coming his way with an extra horse in tow.

When the two got close they reined in, before anything was said, Jake reached back and produced a small bottle of rye and pulled the cork with his teeth then spit it to the ground. Pat sit back not saying a word and waited his turn. Jake handed him the bottle and Pat tipped it back then threw the empty next to the cork.

Both men sat and looked at each other waiting for the other to speak. They both had the same question on their minds. Finally, Jake broke the silence and said, "Same as you. I was too busy to see the bastard ride off but I would bet everything I have I could take you right to him." "We might aughta think on this a while before we ride up to that ranch, don't you agree?" Pat asked. Jake sighed a little and nodded in agreement.

They had two dead men they had to take back to town and loading dead weight onto the back of a horse is better done when one has help. They slowly reined around and returned to where Pat left the dead gunman lying in the red Colorado dirt.

Jake slid out of the saddle and unbuckled the dead man's pistol, then rolled it up and put it in Pat's bags. Pat climbed down and turned out his pockets. Just as before, several gold eagles fell to the dirt. Jake was searching his bags in hopes of finding out his name and found nothing but a forty-one-caliber derringer and a pack of wooden matches wrapped in a cloth rag.

Jake took the gunman by one arm and Pat had the other then they brought him to somewhat of a standing position and slung him face down over the saddle. While Jake was tying him in place, Pat picked his Winchester out of the dirt and looked at it. "This gun is near new," Pat said, he went on went on, "I'll be keeping this," Jake smiled and climbed back into the saddle. Pat mounted up and took the reins of the outlaw's horse and headed back to the road where the other horse waited.

When they reached the road, Pat tied the one horse just as Jake had done and untied the other, then they rode to the body Jake had left behind. Once there, Jake picked up the guns and helped Pat load and tie the other of Crown's gunmen to the saddle.

"What you figure Crown will do now Jake?" Pat asked. "You know Pat, as much as I hate it, we have to ride to that ranch for two reasons. We gotta Crown and you know we ain't gonna do that without going through Latrell," Jake answered. Pat nodded in agreement and climbed into the saddle. Jake tied on the extra rifle and mounted up, then headed back toward La' Junta.

"When we get to town, I'll take care of the horses and get these two planted, you go see the doc," Jake said. Pat stayed quiet. The ride back to LA 'Junta was quick and silent, neither man liked the idea of visiting Crown's ranch. They knew there would be gun play and there was always the chance of a bad ending. Pat's leg was swelled and throbbing although he tried to hide it. They knew they would have to lay up for at least a day because of Pat's leg.

When a bloody US Marshall rode into town with two dead men lashed over their saddles, the people on the boardwalk stopped and watched. Jake and Pat couldn't hear them but they could see them whispering as they rode by. The people didn't know who they were or why they were dead but they saw they were brought in behind a badge.

Pat reached over and passed off the extra reins to Jake then rode to the Doc's office and reined in under his shingle. With great pain, he slowly climbed out of the saddle. Just as his right foot hit the ground, his knee buckled slightly and he let out a heavy sigh. He first tied up his tired horse and stepped into the little office to find he was alone. Pat looked around a little then stepped back onto the boards.

A young boy across the street with a small black dog was floating a homemade boat in a water trough when Pat saw him. "Hey boy," Pat said. The young kid picked up his boat out of the water and looked up at the red headed marshal that was waving to him.

Pat motioned for him to come over and he came running with the little black dog at his side. "You wanna earn a buck?" he asked the red-faced kid. "Yes sir, what do I gotta do to get a dollar?" "You go find the doc and tell him the marshal is at his office and needs to see him," Pat answered. The red-faced kid with the dog at his side and the boat in his hand took off in a dead run down the street toward the saloon.

Jake rode on toward the sheriff's office, knowing it was a common courtesy to keep the sheriff informed. Ted would want to know what went on and if he should expect trouble in town. Jake and Pat still didn't know the names of the men tied across the horses and he hoped Ted might know who they were.

He reined in in front of the office and before he could dismount the big sheriff stepped through the door. Jake swung down out of the saddle and looked at Ted. "They give us no chance Ted, they started shooting as soon as they saw us., Pat's over at the docs getting sewed up, a bullet slid across the top of his leg and cut a nice little ditch in it."

"You see Crown?" he asked. "Yeah, he was there, but he slipped out when all the shooting was going on," Jake said. While Jake was talking to Ted, the white-headed old doctor stepped into his office smelling of whiskey and carrying his black bag. "Boy, I'll bet that really smarts," he said with a taste of humor as he looked down at the bloody groove in Pat's leg. Pat was kind of taken with the old doctor's levity.

While Pat was getting his leg sewed up, Ted was walking around the horses looking at the bodies. Jake had climbed out of the saddle and was tying the young horse to the post when he heard Ted say, "I know this one I think." Jake looked back and saw Ted holding one of the dead men by the hair. "I ain't sure till I see him stretched out, so let's get him over to the undertakers."

The undertaker's place was on the back street not far from the black-smiths and livery stable. When Jake heard the sheriff say this, he started untying the horse carrying the man known to Ted. Ted took the reins of one of the horses and started for the back street. he didn't bother to mount, he walked with the sheriff between the buildings and followed him to the place where he would learn if Ted was right.

Ted was leading one of the horses between the buildings and Jake was following close behind. At a small wood building, Jake saw a hand painted sign hanging above the window telling him they reached their destination. Once there, they secured the horses then started untying bodies. As they were loosening knots, they heard the squeak of rusty hinges and the front door slowly swung open.

Before they saw anyone, they heard someone say, "Bring 'em in here." Jake walked around and helped Ted slide the long-haired dead man to the ground. With each man under a shoulder, they carried the lifeless body through the door and laid him out on an oak table where a tall gaunt apron clad man stood calmly waiting.

Jake stood silently and watched as Ted wiped the long hair out of the dead man's face. Ted looked at him for a long minute, "Yeah that's him, his name is Don Wallace. It's been near ten years, but I still recognize him. His hair was a little darker and he was a deputy sheriff then.

I saw two men pull on him at the same time and he killed 'em both real quick like. Iit was a clean killing, you won't find no paper on him. He was one hell of a gunman in his day, never back shot anyone. He did it straight up and face to face and he knew how to do it," Ted said. Jake got the impression Ted was a little put back seeing his old acquaintance stretched out on the table. Then both men went back to the horses and did as before, dropping the other gunman on the table next to Wallace.

While Jake was with Ted, Pat limped out of the doctor's office and started for the mercantile, he needed new trousers before they started hunting Crown. Once out of the undertaker's office, Jake untied the horses and headed for the livery stable, which was close by.

While Jake was stabling the dead men's

horses, Ted walked back to his office and dropped down at his desk to see Levi hugging the bars. "Now it's my turn Levi," he said. "Tell me about Wallace and what he was doing at the ranch," Ted demanded. Levi could see he was about half pissed and in a bad mood.

"When you gonna let me out of here Ted?" Levi asked. "You ain't leaving here til Pat says to cut you lose," Ted answered. "Now, about Wallace, and don't leave nothing out," Ted said.

'First time I saw Wallace is when Mr. Crown bought the place, he was Crown's security and bodyguard. You never saw him without his guns. Where Mr. Crown went, Don went. He wasn't a bad guy to be around. He didn't speak much, but he did take his job very seriously. Even Luke stepped aside for him. Ted, he wasn't like the others. He wasn't a hired killer, he was a guard and a likeable fellow," Levi said.

CHAPTER

11

Jake tied the young black in front of an overflowing trough sitting in front of the stable then dropped a can of grain for each of the extra horses he and Pat brought in. When he turned to leave the stable, Pat limped in with his gray in tow. He was wearing new gray pants, the bulky bandage wrapped around his leg could not be hidden by the new trousers.

"You ready to ride out to Crown's place?" Jake asked. " Yeah, but I wanna stop by Ted's office. I got a couple questions for Levi first," Pat answered. Jake untied the black stallion and the two walked the short distance to the sheriff's office. When they walked in, Ted was sitting at the desk puffing on a cigar while Levi was sitting on his bunk and sipping a small bottle of cheap whiskey.

"You drinking the prisoners nowadays Ted?" Pat asked. Ted looked up and winked at him. When they looked back at Levi, it was obvious, he was half drunk. Pat walked up and grabbed on to the bars. "Tell me Mr. Boone, if Crown ain't at the ranch, where would he be?" he asked. Jake watched as Levi drained the last of the small bottle and took a deep breath. "Well from the questions Ted here been asking, I figure you two got Wallace and Perry.

Levi hesitated for a long minute, "Well, there's a couple places he could go. I'll bet if he's not at the ranch house he's probably up at that cabin he's got west of the ranch. He goes there fishing and elk hunting quite a bit. He does like his hunting and fishing. If he ain't there, he's probably in Rocky Ford. He has family there," he said, slurring his words. Pat glanced at Jake and grinned slightly. "You want out of here?" he asked Levi. Jake knew exactly what Pat had in mind. Levi got to his feet and staggered slightly, then he took two unsteady steps toward the bars. When he got in reach Pat grabbed him by the shirt and glanced back at Jake.

Jake, who was leaning against the desk, stepped out of the door and headed directly for the livery stable: he had a horse to saddle. Pat pushed Levi back towards the small bunk. "You're gonna get your wish, Levi. You're going for a ride." Wobbling on his feet, Levi grinned slightly and picked up his hat. Twenty minutes later Jake came back through the door with a pair of shiny wrist cuffs in his hand. When Levi saw the cuffs, he then knew what Pat had in mind and he lowered his head. Once snapped on both wrists, Jake pulled open the door and dragged the drunk hostler to the closest water trough. With a hand full of hair, he pushed the drunk man shoulder deep in the murky water.

Water sloshed out of the trough as Levi fought and struggled for a breath of air, trying to get to his feet. When Jake thought he needed air, he pulled him up out of the open tank long enough for him to catch another breath, then pushed and held him back down in the cloudy water.

"Now Levi, you climb up on that horse, and

you're gonna take a ride with us." Still more than half drunk, the soaking wet prisoner climbed into the saddle and looked down at his captor while water dripped out of his hair onto the dry ground below.

"I don't know what you're thinking but I'll tell you this, don't do it, it would be a bad mistake. Any trouble from you and I'll cuff you to a tree and that'll be the last you see of me." Jake looked at him and knew he understood, Levi lowered his head in submission.

When Pat came out of the sheriff's office the first thing, he noticed was Jake had the Sharps tied behind his saddle. He gave it a quick glance and climbed back onto his mount. Jake, anxious to ride, reined around and set a fast pace just shy of a run. Pat nudged Levi to Jake's right side, then he pulled up to his right with the drunk hostler in the middle. This day was half doneand Jake wanted to reach the ranch before the sun dipped below the horizon.

There was still the matter of Luke Latrell. Jake figured if Crown ran, Latrell would be at his side. That's what they both wanted. They wanted Crown in the worst way and the way they saw it,

Latrell would just be a bonus if they got him.

When they reached the place on the side of the hill where the shootout had happened earlier that morning, Jake reined in, keeping Levi close at his side. Pat reached back and took Levi's pistol out of his saddle bags. He dropped the shells to the ground and pushed it back into Levi's holster.

"How does Crown pay you?" Jake asked. Levi, still a little drunk, thought for a moment. "He pays everyone in gold coin, he doesn't like paper," Levi answered. Pat reined his horse around where he could see Levi's face. "Where does he get all that gold he hands out?" Pat asked. Levi grinned big. "He's part owner in one of them silver mines up by Carson City in Nevada. He converts his paper to silver and gold coin.

Jake looked at Pat, "Be on your toes from here in," Jake said. With a slight touch of the iron, the horses moved to a trot. They kept up that pace until they came to where they left the road earlier that day and Jake reined in; Pat followed with Levi still in-between.

"Give me that glass of yours, Pat." When Pat handed Jake the glass, he tapped it on his leg and said. "Keep to the left side a little." Pat looked at him with question. When Jake reined left and rode to the top of the hill Pat knew exactly what he meant and why he brought the Plains rifle.

Pat looked at Levi and said, "Move out. You try to run, I'll kill ya." Levi could tell Pat meant every word he said. He touched his horse and rode around the base of the hill where the road lined up with the front of Crown's house. Anyone who looked could tell Levi was scared to the point he couldn't hide it.

"We ride in there they'll kill us both," he said. Then he looked back to the tree covered hill where he knew Jake to be. Slowly, they approached, looking in all directions. Pat held his reins in his left and his right rode the black holster at his side. Just before they reined in, the screen door opened with a loud squeak. Pat quickly drew the pistol and both men pulled to a stop. Levi was to Pat's right and several feet to his rear.

Long before they reached the house, Jake tied up the young black horse and pulled the plains rifle from his saddle. He fed one of the big bullets in the gun, Then he stretched the looking glass and dropped into a sitting position. With the long- rifle across his lap, he peered through the glass searching for anything. As he searched, he noticed a narrow, well-used trail that looked like it ran out of the barn and faded into the pines just beyond the house.

What followed the squeak was a large black woman with a white bandana tied around her head and wearing a light blue house dress covered with a plaid apron. She stepped through the door wiping her hands on her apron.

Jake, with the glass pressed to his eye, searched for anything. Cautiously ,he watched the woman step onto the porch. When she saw his badge, she said. "Is there something I can help you with Marshall? did you go get yourself in trouble Levi?" Jake, not being able to hear her words, knew she was of little danger.

Moving the glass from left to right he searched. Suddenly, he saw on the right side of the bunkhouse a man was carrying a rifle moving slowly and staying close to the wall. Jake knew from where Pat and Levi sat; they couldn't see the oncoming rifleman.

Eerie of their situation, Pat, along with Levi, looked from side to side as the woman spoke.

When it was totally evident the unknown rifleman was trying to get into a surprise position, Jake picked up the long gun and slid the rear sight up to the five-hundred-yard mark and laid the rifle between his knees. He returned the long glass to his eye and watched the man with the rifle get closer.

When the gunman was at the corner of the bunk house which was fifty yards from Pat, Jake lowered the glass and pressed the rifle to his shoulder. Peeping through the little hole, Jake knew he had him. *Maybe if he sees Pat is wearing a badge, he'll lower the gun,* he thought.

"No Miss Ida, I ain't in no trouble," Levi answered. "Is anyone in the house with you?" Pat demanded. Just then, the rifleman stepped around the corner and raised the rifle. "Lower the gun," Jake said to himself. "Forest Crown here?" Pat asked the housekeeper. Before she could answer Pat's questions, she heard a loud whap sound closely followed by the distant crack of a rifle.

In the blink of an eye, Pat leapt out of the saddle and filled his hand with iron. When his feet hit the ground, his knees buckled from the pain.

At the same time, Levi, still cuffed, jumped to the ground, and laid there face down. When the smoke cleared, Jake could see the rifleman was no longer on his feet, the rifle he carried was still at his fingertips.

Quickly, Pat glanced back at Levi lying in the dirt and saw he was no problem. Now squatting low, Pat turned and searched in all directions but he still could not see from his position the rifleman lying face down.

The frightened housekeeper darted back into the house followed by the squeak and slam of the door. Jake, with the glass back to his eye, scanned back and forth. Seeing nothing, he quickly dropped the scope in his bags and leaped into the saddle, the long gun still in his grip.

Jake set his spurs and the young black reluctantly bowed to the commands of his rider. In a cloud of dust, he road between the trees and off the face of the hill and back down to the rode that would deliver him directly in front of the Crown ranch. In less than three minutes, the young black brought Jake to Pat's side.

By the time Jake reined in Pat was standing over the lifeless body of an unknown gunman. Pat looked down at the rifle to see it was cocked, then he noticed the short Mexican jacket. He saw the sugarloaf sombrero hanging on a lanyard then he noticed the gold front tooth Meeks had told him of. When Pat saw the gold tooth, he knew Jake had saved his life.

"Levi, get over here," Pat said in a demanding tone. Levi, who was still cuffed and back on his feet, walked and brushed dirt off his pants as he made his way to where Jake and Pat stood looking down at the dead gunman. "Who is this guy? Can you put a name to him?' Jake asked.

"I don't know his real name Marshall, all I ever heard him called was Pacos. Mr. Crown brought him out of Carson City, he was part of security at one of them mines, I think." Pat squatted down and turned out his pockets. Finding nothing but two gold eagles, Pat got to his feet while Jake leaned over and unbuckled the dead man's pistol that was still lashed down in the holster.

Without a word, the two angry men headed for the house. When they pulled the door open, they saw the nervous housekeeper standing in the kitchen. "Where is Crown?" Pat demanded. What caught Jake's eye was a rifle rack on the wall to his left. Jake with a hand full of Colt, walked up to the rack that covered nearly half the wall.

"I don't know where they are. Mr. Crown, he just come in and took two of them guns and some bullets and told Mr. Latrell they had to get saddled and he needed a fresh horse. Mr. Latrell saddled them horses and got some bed rolls then they rode off." The nervous housekeeper said as she pointed to the back of the house.

Jake looked at Pat, "Levi get in here," Jake hollered. It was less than a minute when Levi, who was still cuffed, opened the screen door and stepped in. Before the door could slammed Jake called him to the rack.

"There's two missing out of here, what's gone?" he snapped. Levi looked for a minute, "I think a coach gun," then he looked at Pat, "and his real pretty Henry like you carry, Marshall," he answered. "Back on your horse Levi," Pat said, and Levi left the way he came in. In a lower tone Jake asked Pat. "Will your leg let you take a ride like this Pat?" "Yeah, I got no problem there," Pat answered.

Jake stepped out on the porch ahead of Pat

and stopped, then spoke in almost a whisper. "I don't want to ride up to that cabin blind, so I figure we'll take Levi with us as far as the cabin." "Pat, why don't you go back in there and get us some grub, I'll get blankets and we'll run that old man and his guard dog to the ground." Pat agreed with a smile and a nod then went back in the house.

Jake climbed in the saddle took Levi's reins and headed the short distance to the bunk house. When he reined in, he slid out of the saddle and told Levi "Climb down. "You're gonna be needing some blankets for the trip unless you wanna sleep in the cold dirt."

"Hold it Jake, you don't need me, I can tell you how to get there. They see me with you, I'm dead and you know it." "Well, you better pray they don't see ya, cause you're our guide, like it or not," Jake said. Hearing this the unwilling hostler looked to the ground and knew he didn't have a choice.

Levi slowly dismounted and started to walk into the bunk house when Jake stopped him and pulled his pistol. With a signal from Jake, Levi stepped aside and Jake stood back and kicked the door open, then moved in to make sure he was alone.

"Come on in and make a bed roll Levi and don't dawdle, we've got to ride," Jake said. Levi slowly walked in and pulled the blankets off the first two cots he saw. He rolled them up and tied them to the back of his saddle. Jake followed him out with an arm load of blankets and climbed onto the waiting horse.

When they got back to the front of the house, Pat was tying a white cloth bag to his saddle. Jake climbed out of the saddle and tossed Pat two blankets then walked to the porch and began to roll the blankets he'd taken from the bunk house.

Once back in the saddle, Jake looked at Levi. "How far is it to that cabin?" Jake asked. "About four or five hours," he replied. Jake looked to the sky, Pat flipped open the face on his watch. " We can't make it before sundown," Pat said. "You get us close to that cabin before sundown or you'll sleep hog tied," Jake said.

Chapter

12

The Crown ranch sat on the edge of a narrow, grass filled valley in the shadow of a pine covered mountain. On the front side of this valley set the tree covered hill Jake had just ridden down. A narrow, meandering creek ran through the center of the grassy field, making it perfect for grazing cattle.

To the side and back a little sat the bunkhouse like most ranches and farms in Colorado that were big enough to have extra hands. A white wooden silo, standing twenty feet tall, cast a shadow over the bunk house. Directly, behind the house sat a well-cared for, whitewashed barn connected to a large corral.

Next to that, a slow turning windmill pumped water into a round wooden tank, green moss grew on the side under a constant overflow of water. At the back of the barn, that well beaten trail Jake had seen and wondered about faded into the tall pines beyond the house.

Jake reined around and started the up hill climb, he knew this trail would be rough on the horses. Pat motioned to Levi to get in behind Jake then he pulled in behind the hostler. The barn was still in sight when he looked down and saw the fresh tracks from a pair of fast-moving horses. For a moment he reined in, from atop his horse he studied the fresh tracks.

The prints of the two horses were cut deep but there was something odd and he couldn't quite put his finger on. Pat rode around Levi to Jake's side and looked. "They're on the move, they won't be able to run 'em up this mountain they'll have to slow down? Pat said.

Jake said nothing he just studied the ground. He didn't feel right, *Maybe I'm being too careful*, he thought. He looked around a little more, then motioned for Levi to take the lead, "I like you where I can see you," he said. Levi pulled around and set the pace as they climbed. Jake touched the black with his spurs and moved in behind him.

Jake felt uneasy, as they rode his eyes never left the trail. The dusty route followed started getting steeper as they rode. After a couple hours of an uphill climb, Jake rode to Levi's side and grabbed his reins. "I want to know where this cabin is," Jake said in an angry tone. With his hands still cuffed, Levi pointed up towards a peak that looked to be several miles from where they now sat. "At the base of that mountain in a grove of aspens., I've been there a dozen times," he said.

Now deep into the trees, the smell of fresh pine filled the cool air. There wasn't a cloud in the sky, It was cooler up here and they knew they would need the blankets they had tied behind their saddles. As the trail weaved between the big pines, they rode in the dark, where they were rarely touched by the sun.

On both sides of the trail everything was covered by thick layers upon layers of brown pine needles that marked the seasons of many, years gone by. The only ground that wasn't blanketed was the narrow trail they rode.

With a nod of his head, Jake ordered Levi to pick up the pace. The higher they got, the narrower the trail became. The tracks they followed were deep and cut up. Jake could tell Crown's horses were beginning to tire and had begun to slow the same as theirs now were.

The sun was half below the unseen horizon and the dark began to fill the forest when Levi reined in. Jake rode to his side. "A little bit further and the hunting cabin will be in sight, and I'm not coming out of these trees first," Levi said. Pat reined around in front of Levi, "Now you ride that horse," he said then nudged his gray forward with Levi was close behind.

They rode less than a hundred yards when he spotted the stand of aspens. Like Levi said, the cabin sat in the middle of the white bark trees. Immediately, Pat turned his horse around and rode back into the shadows.

Jake climbed out of the saddle and tied his horse to some pine boughs, Pat tying up next to him. Jake looked at Levi, "Get off that horse," he said, then he pulled the glass out of Pat's bags. Pat pulled his Winchester from his scabbard and motioned Levi to follow.

Jake walked between the thick trees keeping out of sight of the cabin as much as possible. When he and Pat found a small opening where he could get a clear view of the aspens, he stretched the scope. What he saw first was the dim, yellow light coming from the only window in the cabin. The light was fading fast and he knew he had but minutes until total darkness.

With the glass pressed to his eye he hunted. There was a slight breeze on his face when he saw the small, secluded cabin. Nearly one thousand yards off, Jake saw the little building with one window and a door in the middle. On the right side, a corral made of lodge-pole pines set about twenty feet from the log cabin.

Through the glass he saw two horses in the small corral and to his surprise, he smelled before he saw the pale gray smoke coming from a stove pipe. Back and forth he scanned for any movement, hoping to see Crown. He then he handed Pat the glass, and watched him put it to his eye, quickly spotting the dim light coming from the lone window.

With the last bit of light, he could barely see the two horses, or the saddle and bridal on the top rail of the corral above a water trough.

Jake hadn't gotten over the feeling something wasn't right about the trail he followed. He passed it off due to the fact he was hunting a ruthless killer who rode through several states and territories for more than ten years killing numerous men, and no one dared to call him.

Pat folded up the scope and walked back in the dark with Jake and Levi to where the tired horses waited. Something didn't seem right about this whole deal. *Something doesn't figure,* Jake thought.

"We should move back a short piece to make sure they don't see the reflection of our fire," Jake said. He took his reins and, along with Pat and Levi, turned and walked back down the trail until they were sure they were safe.

Pat took the heavy cloth bag he had taken from Crown's house and tossed it to Jake. "No jerky for us, we're eating good tonight," Pat said as Jake opened the bag. In the dark he couldn't see it, but he could smell the ham. "Hey, Ida was glad to give it to us, to get me out of her kitchen," he said with a laugh.

Jake and Levi started gathering and breaking sticks for firewood. Not only did they need the light of the fire to stave off the total darkness, but they were also hungry and wanted a cup of coffee.

Once the fire was going, Pat produced a bottle of whiskey and rolled out his blankets then quickly stretched out. He had been in the saddle all day and his leg throbbed. He slipped down his trousers and slowly dripped the whisky on the blood-stained bandage that covered the wound.

Jake looked at him when he heard him moan with pain. Levi sat down and waited; he didn't know whether to ask for food or wait until it was offered. Jake reached down and pulled the knife from his boot, cutting off two big slices of ham, He handed one to Pat. Levi watched and hoped he was next. Jake knew Levi was hungry, so he passed the other slice to the handcuffed man.

Jake took a drink of the whiskey and laid back on his blanket. He still hadn't figured out what troubled him, he just knew something was wrong. The men were dog-tired and silence hovered over camp.

Jake satin silence sipping a cup of trail coffee, thinking. *The smoke he smelled, the soft light from the window, the two horses in the corral. The saddle hanging on the corral.* Then it hit him, and he knew.

Two horses, one saddle, Crown had a spare. We followed three horses in line up that trail, that's why the trail was so cut up. One of the horses must have left the path, he thought.

After a few minutes, he sat up to see Pat stirring the fire with a stick, Levi was leaned against his saddle sipping hot, bitter coffee. " You figure it out Jake?" Pat asked. "Pat, he pulled one over on us. You know why the trail was so cut up?" Jake asked. "It did look mighty cut up," Pat answered. Levi laid back in silence and listened. "We followed three horses up here, one of them left the trail and we never saw it in those thick pine needles."

"There's only one man at the cabin and I'm guessing it's Latrell." Pat stopped stirring for a moment. "Levi, didn't you say he had kin by Rocky Ford?" Pat asked. "Yeah, he's got a cousin or a brother there something like that," Levi answered.

"That's only fifteen miles from La 'Junta. I'll bet he's heading for his kin, they'll help 'em," Jake said. "We can be on his trail in the morning, Jake," Pat said. "Yeah, we can, after I deal with Mr. Latrell," Jake replied.

With nothing else said, the two laid back and fell into a deep sleep. Levi fell asleep wondering what the morning would bring for him. he One thing he knew is he didn't want any part of Luke Latrell

Jake awoke to the snap of Pat breaking small twigs. He sat up just as Pat struck a match with his fingernail. When he touched the match to the twigs, a yellow fire began to grow. Pat took out his watch and flipped open the face. Needing the light, he leaned towards the small flames. "It's just a little past four, Jake." he said.

The morning was cool, the only sound was that of the magpies and the whispering of the breeze through the pines. The smell of smoke was welcome, that meant coffee and something to chew on. Jake stuffed his pistol in his holster and pulled on his boots. Pat reached in his bags and took out a cloth sack and threw Jake a biscuit. Jake stuck a small stick through it and held it over the fire for a moment. Pat watched him. "It makes 'em a little softer sometimes," he said. Pat passed around the canteen and they filled their cups and set them to boil.

Jake took a generous pinch of coffee and dropped it in his cup and waited for the welcome smell to fill his nose. Levi sat up and waited for Pat to toss him one of those hard biscuits. With the second dip in the bag, Pat produced a biscuit and tossed it to Levi.

The three men sat in the dark and sipped the hot coffee, Levi dipped the hard biscuit in the hot coffee. What Levi didn't know was Jake and Pat weren't going to be there at sunup. Jake hadn't seen him, but all his instincts told him Latrell was in that cabin and he was going to take him.

"What you got in mind Jake? I can tell something is stirring around in there," Pat said. "I'm going to be waiting at his front door when the sun comes up," Jake answered. Pat smiled and looked at him. "I want you to make sure he stays here, when we go down there, "he said as he nodded toward the hostler. Pat looked at Levi.

"I'll wait right here as long as I don't gotta

go down there," Levi said, nodding towards Levi. "Oh I know you'll be here," Pat said.

Pat was chewing on a piece of ham when he got to his feet and started saddling his gray. Jake threw a blanket over the black and then topped it with his saddle while Levi watched. "You might wanna get saddled Levi," Pat said. Still cuffed, Levi did as he was told.

Pat reached in his bags and threw Levi a pair of hobbles. "Put 'em on that horse you're riding," he said. Jake knew what Pat was doing, it was Levi that had no idea what Pat had in mind. Once the hobbles were on, Pat told him to mount up.

Levi slowly, climbed into the saddle of the hobbled horse. Pat walked over and unlocked one side of the cuffs and pulled the loose end through the hole just below the pommel. He snapped the cuff back onto Levi's wrist, leaving him cuffed to the saddle on a horse that couldn't walk, let alone run.

"Now I know you'll be here when we get back," Jake said. He laughed slightly and climbed into the saddle then Pat mounted up and moved to Jake's side. "We're going out across that little clearing and coming up on the back of that cabin. When he comes out, I'll be there," Jake said.

Under the cover of darkness Jake touched his horse and moved out with Pat at his side. With no moon, the only light was that of the stars. When they came to the edge of the little meadow, Jake reined in. It was early, but they looked for a light in the cabin. Seeing none, they moved toward the left end of the aspen grove.

By the time they crossed the meadow a slight splinter of light peaked over the horizon, reflecting off the white bark of the trees. They rode with caution as they approached the little log house. Fifty yards from their target, they tied up their mounts and hoped the horses would remain silent.

The ground was covered with a thick layer of dry aspen leaves that cracked under their boots as they walked, still they moved as silently as possible. Now with the light in their favor, they neared the back of the house as the light quickly filled the meadow they just rode over. "You sit here Pat, I'll be between the house and the corral. I'm gonna try to draw him out," Jake said in a whisper. Pat with a hand full of Winchester, replied with a simple nod.

By the time, the two reached the cabin they could see a yellow glow on the ground in front of the house. Pat moved through the thick leaves and found himself up against the log wall. Catfooted Jake walked the length of the cabin and appeared between the cabin and the corral.

Next to the wall sat a short stump that had been cut off clean. Silently, Jake loosened his Colt in his holster and sat down on the stump, waiting and listening.

He hadn't sat long when he caught the first sniff of smoke that he knew to be from the wood stove. By this hour, the sun filled the clearing and lit the trees on the other side of the meadow. An hour hadn't passed, when Jake thought he could hear movement on the other side of the wall.

Quietly, he got up and walked to the corral, swung the gate open and returned to the log where he sat. After a moment, he reached down and picked up a stick, tossing it at the horses as they drank. Pat stepped forward and took a quick glance as the horses briskly fled the small corral.

Jake hoped Luke would see the horses and step out onto the plank porch. He also knew a man like Luke Latrell, who had always lived by his wits and his gun, would never go anywhere, or do anything without his weapon.

Shortly, after the horses walked by the only window, Jake heard the squeak of the door and a pair boots on the plank porch. Jake knew if he heard the boots so did Pat. With his gun loose in his holster, Jake stepped around the corner into the open.

There stood the shirtless killer Luke Latrell. His black high crowned hat blocked his eyes from the sun. He had a short, neatly trimmed black moustache that highlighted the shadow of a beard. This was the first time Jake saw Luke Latrell and he could see; Luke wasn't a slouch. He stood a little over six feet tall with broad shoulders and heavily muscled arms. When he turned and saw Jake, Jake could tell Luke was ready to do battle. Men like Latrell were always ready for a fight. He was a professional gunman and this was the way of life for Luke.

Standing at a slight angle, his left hand was in plain sight, but his right was behind his leg. There he stood looking into the dark eyes of the young gunman Jake Cleary. Pat stood silently at his back with a Winchester trained on him. He had no idea that if he did beat Jake by chance or by skill, he would die anyway. Jake had his hat pulled down to block the early sun. He couldn't tell if Luke's right hand was empty or full of iron, but every instinct in his body told him it was iron.

Silently, two strong, equal gun fighters measured each other. As they studied the other, Jake saw a slight squint in Luke's eyes. He knew then, Luke would make his play.

Quicker than the blink of an eye, Luke's iron filled hand started up just before Jake's hand flashed for his gun. Jake's barrel had barely cleared leather, when two shots echoed through the mountains. Instantly, Luke was slammed back against the wall, his hands flew up and his Colt tumbled to the ground.

The bullet had drilled its way through Luke's stomach and out his back, blowing blood all over the pine door. Commanded by instinct and a touch of fear, Jake re-cocked the Colt for a second shot. Seeing Luke tumble forward in the dirt, he relaxed the hammer and holstered his gun. Pat, seeing that Luke was still alive and clawing at the dirt trying to reach his gun, stepped forward and kicked the Colt aside.

Luke was still alive when Jake bent down and rolled him over. "Where is Crown, tell me where Crown is!" Jake demanded. Luke slowly opened his eyes and looked into the dark eyes of the first man who had ever beaten his draw, then his lips tried to form two words.

He could see Luke was straining to talk. In a breathy tone, Luke whispered twice, "the Razor," then coughed a little blood and his eyes slowly closed. Jake confused looked up at Pat, what did he mean, the Razor then he lowered Latrell to the ground and got to his feet.

Pat looked away, as though lost in thought. "That rings a bell, Jake," Pat said, then he picked up the killer's gun and handed it to Jake. Jake rolled the gun over and over in his hand before the seventeen notches on the wood grips caught his eye.

Pat could see Jake was a little nervous. "You know, Jake, his bullet buried itself between your feet, I saw the dirt." Jake nodded and tucked the gun into his belt then said, "I'll go get our horses."

CHAPTER

13

While Jake walked to where the horses were tied, Pat turned out Luke's pockets to find three double eagles and a gold watch. He flipped open the face of the watch and wasn't at all surprised when he saw a faded picture of a young pretty woman fixed inside the lid of the time piece.

He looked at the watch and mumbled to himself, "You died at six thirty-five." Then he closed the watch and walked into the cabin looking for the gunman's saddlebags. What he needed was some kind of proof; that it was Luke Latrell lying on the porch in the pool of blood.

The first thing he saw was the well engraved Henry rifle that Levi had described laying on the table with his saddlebags and a box of bullets. Pat immediately started rifling through the bags: what he found was a bird's head Colt with a half box of ammunition. The bird's head Colt was a self cocking Colt that was smaller in overall size than the Peace Maker he died with.

In the other side he found an old, yellowed envelope addressed to Luke Latrell, general delivery, Tombstone, Arizona. That was all he needed to secure the reward money. When he stepped out on the porch, Jake rode up leading Pat's gray mare.

"Let's round up those horses and get Luke loaded up then get on Crown's trail," Jake said. Pat climbed into the saddle and handed Jake Luke's Winchester, Jake looked at it and slid it in Pat's bedroll. Slowly, they walked to the grazing horses. Once they had Luke tied over the buckskin, the two men, with two horses in tow, started across the open field.

Halfway across the field, Pat reined in with Jake at his side and reached into his shirt pocket to hand Jake the watch Luke carried. As he handed it to Jake he said, "The Razor. If I remember right, it's a cattle ranch about a day's ride west of Rocky Ford. It's a pretty fair spread."

Jake flipped open the watch and quickly glanced at it, then he looked at Pat. "Well, now I know where we're heading," Jake said. Then he went on. "Pat, we been chasing this crumb long enough, it's time we put an end to this run." Jake replied. "We can cut this chase short," Pat said. Jake's head snapped around, "What's your thinking, Pat?" he asked.

"We know he turned off the trail. There's nothing that way but mountains between here and there. If we hightail it back to his ranch and grab a couple fresh mounts, we can be sleeping in Rocky Ford tonight," Pat said. Jake smiled slightly and once again, the two set their spurs headed for where Levi waited.

When they got back into the shade of

the trees, they saw Levi within a few feet of where they left him. Jake climbed out of the saddle and started rolling up his blanket. Pat went over and unlocked the cuffs that kept Levi secured to the horse. "Get 'em rolled up if you're gonna keep 'em," Pat said to Levi.

Levi walked over and saw Luke tied face down over the bloody saddle and blood dripping to the ground. " I heard the shooting, it sounded like one shot from here," Levi said. Jake looked at the hostler and kept tying.

"Pat, we gotta get some grass and water for these horses," Jake commented. "About halfway down there's a spot of grass where that little stream crosses the trail. When we get to the ranch we can feed 'em proper," Pat said, then he told Levi to mount up. Once Levi was in the saddle, Pat tied Luke's buckskin to the back of his saddle.

Jake touched his horse and started back down the trail while Pat climbed in the saddle. Once atop the horse he told Levi,

"You follow and keep up." Levi did as he was told and reined in behind Pat. By this time Jake was fifty yards ahead of them and closely watching the ground as he rode.

Twenty minutes down the trail Pat was still behind Jake. Pat watched as Jake reined in and climbed down from the black horse. With his reins in hand, Jake slowly faded out of sight into the trees. Pat rode up to where Jake dismounted and reined in and waited. Levi rode up behind him. "Where'd he go?" he asked. Pat just acted as though he heard nothing.

Little time had passed before Jake rode back to where Pat waited. " This is where he left the trail, Pat. Go on ahead I'm gonna follow a while and see what I can, I'll catch up with ya," Jake said, then he reined around and rode back into the darkness of the tall trees.

Pat touched his horse and began to move back down the steep trail. The trip back down was faster and much easier on the horses. Whenever he saw any greenery, he would rein in and let the horses forage on the little grass that grew in the dark of the trees. Jake had been gone nearly an hour when Pat came to the small creek that crossed the trail.

He had reined in and was letting the thirsty horses drink when he looked up and saw Jake. Seeing Pat at the creek, he slowed his horse and walked to the little stream of water. "What did you find Jake?" Pat asked. Jake climbed out of the saddle and dropped to his knees and started drinking out of the stream next to his horse.

"I stayed on his trail about a mile. He's riding into more of what we just rode out of. I could see from up top, parts of a trail here and there. "He knows where he's going. The way I figure it, we'll beat him there." Jake answered. Pat smiled and let his horses pick at what little grass was there.

After a few minutes, Jake remounted and rode to Pat's side. At this time, Levi wasn't of much concern to them so they paid little to no attention to him as he rode in their tracks. Jake leaned forward and patted the black horse on the neck. "You know Pat, this horse gets better and better all the time," he said.

Pat chewed on a toothpick and never spoke. After a couple hours, they rode out of the shadows and into the light. The first thing they saw was the tall, white, silo at the Crown ranch, and four of Crown's horses watching them approach. Seeing the ranch, the pace seemed to quicken a little.

About five hundred yards from the corrals and barn they pulled their horses to a dead stop. Jake looked at Pat and gave him a head signal and Pat reined left with the spare in tow and his rifle in hand. Jake loosened his Colt in the holster and turned right, then circled the ranch house keeping out of rifle range, Pat did the same.

Levi watched them momentarily ride out of sight then reappear at the front of the main house. After several minutes, they rode to the back of the house only now, Pat had his rifle holstered. Feeling safe, Levi now nudged his mount into the back of the barn. Before Levi could get out of the saddle, Jake walked up. "No need to get down, you see these two horses get watered when you take Luke here to the sheriff. Do everything like I told you and all will be forgotten." he said. Levi, looking down from atop his horse, agreed with a nod.

Pat then walked up and handed Levi the letter he found in Luke's bags. "You give this to Ted, he'll know what to do with it. Remember Jake's got a big bounty coming, so do this right or there'll be a poster on you in a week." Levi nodded and rode out of the barn and past the house.

They dropped the saddles on the black and gray and led their hungry mounts to a stack of hay inside the barn. The hungry horses buried their noses in the sweet grass. Jake found a wooden bin full of oats and dropped grain for both horses while Pat looked over the horses that walked the large corral.

With a rope in one hand and a can of grain in the other, Jake coaxed a red mare close enough to slip a loop over her head and lead her into the shade of the barn. Pat took the can and soon both men were saddling two of Crown's horses while their mounts fed and watered.

Just as Jake finished tightening the cinch on the horse he commandeered, one of Crown's hand's stepped into the shade of the barn. Jake's hand quickly dropped to his gun and at the same time, Pat stepped from around the horse he was saddling. Instantly, the ranch hand stopped in his tracks when he saw Jake poised for a fight.

"I'm Pat Brennon, US Marshall. We're borrowing these mounts and we'll return 'em on the way back," he said. Then Pat walked up and shook hands with young cowboy. "I'm Jake Cleary, we shouldn't have these horses long, it's just ours are played out and we got a fair ride ahead of us," he said. Then Pat reached in his pocket and produced one of the gold double eagles he took from Luke.

"What's your name?" he asked. "I'm Al Cutler Marshall, he answered. "Well Al, you see these two mounts?" he asked as he pointed to Jake's horse and his gray. He handed the young ranch hand the double eagle. "While we're gone, I want you to take care of these two horses like they were yours. I want them fed and grained and no one rides 'em, and this twenty is yours," he said. The young hand smiled and looked at the horses.

"Yes, sir Marshall, just like their mine. I'll do like you ask," he replied then he went on, "That looked like Luke's horse, Marshall. Was that Luke tied across the saddle I seen just now?" "he asked. "Yeah, that was Luke," Pat answered. Then he and Jake mounted up and the two rode out of the barn on Forest Crowns horses.

It was a little past midday when they turned back onto the main road that would take them to Rocky Ford and a night off the ground. Where the road to Crown's ranch tied in with the road to Rocky Ford, they reined in.

Pat stood in the saddle and took another gold coin out of his pocket, handing it to Jake. "This was Luke's," Pat said. Jake took the coin and spoke. "Let's go get a room. I wanna send a wire to Jodie."

They had been away from their wives for some time now, and their way of life had changed when their women rolled out of town, all because of Forest Crown. Now he was on the run and Jake and Pat, both knew it was just a matter of days until they rode Crown into the ground.

Once on the road to Rocky Ford, they could barely see Levi as he hightailed it back to town. After three hours of hard riding, the little farming town of Rocky Ford, Colorado was in sight. They were tired hungry and the horses needed fed as bad as they did. Slowly, they looked around as they rode into the east end of town. Pat took the badge from his shirt and slipped it into his pocket.

Jake hadn't been in Rocky Ford since before he left home for the army and the last time Pat was in town, he was here for a hanging six months earlier. Now they were here to put an end to the man that had uprooted their lives and had gotten Pat shot in the leg. When they rode in, they went directly to the livery stable. their second stop was Ceili's café and finally, a bed up off the ground.

"Jake, you ever met Ceil?' Pat asked. Jake answered no with a shake of his head. "Well, she's a cute little red headed Irish gal. "The last time I was in her place eating, a half-drunk drover didn't want to pay for his meal. He got into an argument with Ceili over the bill and started to manhandle her.

Well, she reaches in her apron pocket and pulls out a little single shot, derringer. It took both hands for her to cock the gun, then she shot him right through the top of the foot. While he's hopping around bellowing, she pushed him down and took the money out of his pocket. I sat there and watched the whole thing," Pat said in a hysterical laughter as they walked to the café. Hearing this story Jake broke out in full laughter. "Over a steak, huh," he said. Pat was laughing so hard he couldn't answer.

After a hot meal, the two walked into the White Goose, the only saloon in town. Jake looked around, he noticed most everyone was wearing brogans. Only one or two drinkers were openly armed giving the impression it was peaceful little town.

Pat, who was carrying his Winchester, went directly to the bar where he dropped a dollar and got a half empty bottle of whiskey with two glasses. The White Goose looked like all saloons in Colorado. The wood plank floor that needed the street mud pushed back to where it came from, and the big, cracked mirror behind the bar. Several tables with uneven legs were strung about the room and oil lamps with soot covered chimneys were hanging from the tin covered ceiling. As usual several brass, spittoons sat at the base of the bar. As always skimpy dressed hostesses were there to separate the customers from their money.

Pat sat down and poured Jake a glass of the brown whiskey The two looked around. "Let's see who will be first," Pat said, Jake grinned. He finished his first and started filling Pat's glass, when he looked up.

"It's the short, top heavy red head," Jake said, like he was announcing the winner of a contest. The pretty young lady came to their table with a smile and said, " Hi I'm Carmen. Who's gonna buy me a drink?" she cheerfully asked. "Grab a glass and a seat, Carmen, I'll buy you a drink," Pat said.

This pretty, young hostess was wearing a blue satin dress that hung just above her knees. Her perfect red hair was done up with a blue ribbon on the top of her head and her lips were the color of a ripe cherry. The low cut of the blue dress made it look as though part of her was about to explode out the top of that shiny dress.

She quickly appeared with a glass and sat down next to Pat. "I don't think I've ever seen you two. What are you boys doing in town?" she asked. "We heard the Razor is doing some hiring and we're looking for work," Jake said. Pat took a sip of the cheap whiskey and set his glass down. "How far is it to the Razor from here?" Pat asked. "I haven't ever been there myself, but I know when the hands come in on payday, they always spend the night." Pat just nodded.

When the saloon girl realized, she wasn't going to make any money from these two drifters she said thanks for the drink and left them to sip their whiskey. They sat there another hour sipping whiskey and listening to the same old tunes being pounded out on the untuned piano.

It was about eight o'clock when the door swung open and the town sheriff walked in. For a moment he just looked around. When he saw Pat, he smiled and headed directly for their table.

"Here comes Able," Pat said in a low tone. The big sheriff walked up and grabbed a chair and turned it around before dropping down in it, resting his arms on the back.

"Hello Pat, how long has it been? I heard about the trouble in Las Animas.

Who's your friend here?" he asked with an air of confidence. "Able, this is Jake Cleary, and that trouble you mentioned is what brought us here." Able just looked at Jake and nodded as to say hi.

The sheriff a big burley fellow, he had big hairy arms jutting out of the sleeves on his faded blue shirt that were rolled up halfway to his elbows. He wore a sweat stained hat pushed back on his head and he had big, brawny hands that looked like sunbaked leather. The double-barreled sawed-off shotgun he laid across the top of the table let everyone know his smile was deceiving.

"I'm betting you and Jake here got some questions for me, don't you Pat?" Pat just smiled and poured him a drink in Carmen's glass. "Yeah, we do Able. We're chasing a fella name Forest Crown and we believe he's headed for the Razor. We think he's got kin there and we want him bad," Pat said.

"What makes you think he headed there?" Able asked. "Well yesterday, Jake here killed Luke Latrell." Able's head quickly snapped around and looked at Jake. "With his last breath he said Crown was headed for the Razor, so here we are." "You know where the Razor is Pat?" "That's one of the questions we had for ya," Pat said. Jake sat in silence never taking his eyes off the big, gruff sheriff. "Yeah, it's a day's ride west of here to the house, but you're on the Razor long before you get to the house," he answered.

"You know Forest Crown?" Pat asked. "No, but I've heard of him. I don't know if he's kin to the Cutters or not. I know he rides with a lot of muscle and What I've heard of him I don't like," Able answered. I think its best I ride out there with you tomorrow," he added.

"Well, I appreciate your offer Able, but me and Jake here can handle it. You just point us in the right direction and we'll find the ranch," Pat said. "Ok Pat, I tried. You ride west out of here about three miles and take the left road. You can't miss it, the ruts are deep. Just keep going, once you get past the dry spot, you'll start seeing grass and cattle and sheep all the way to the house," Able added. "Sheep," Jake commented. "Yeah, the dammedest thing I ever saw and these are cattle people," Able said then he looked at Jake. "Jake I gotta know how you took Latrell?"

Jake took the last sip out of his glass and looked at the big sheriff. "It was straight up sheriff; his hand was full of iron when he saw me. He was overconfident and I was just faster," Jake answered, then he got to his feet. "I want to see a soft bed now," he said in a tired voice, then he reached out to shake the sheriff's hand. Pat nodded at the sheriff and left with Jake.

CHAPTER

14

Jake was awake when the early morning sun came crashing through the window in his small room. Without a thought, he pounded on the wall to wake Pat. No one had told him and he didn't dream it, he didn't know how he knew but he knew today this hunt would come to an end one way or another.

He walked over and looked in the mirror a second before scratching his chin and splashing a little cold water on his face out of the porcelain pan that sat on the little box dresser. Jake walked out of the room strapping on his pistol while he headed directly for the café that sat across the street. He was hungry and tired and wanted to put an end to this chase. He didn't like sleeping alone and eating biscuits that were hard as bullets and chewing on dried meat. He wanted a plate of runny eggs, a wheel of ham and some hot biscuits with a pot of coffee he didn't have to make.

When he stepped out on the boardwalk, he didn't look back. He knew Pat was right behind him carrying that rifle. He walked across the street and into Ceili's café where he took a corner table knowing Pat would lean his rifle in the corner.

They sat in silence for a moment and waited for the cups to be delivered. Once the coffee was poured, Jake got a slight smile. "We'll get him today, I know it." Pat, not saying a word, was glad to hear this because in the past, Jake was usually right.

This was a good morning for Jake, he got his runny eggs and ham and potatoes he didn't plan on. He knew deep down in his soul that, before sunset, the hunt for Forest

Crown would be over. They both ate like they hadn't eaten in days and swilled down hot coffee as fast as they could drink it then left as fast as they come. Now they had horses to saddle and they were both in a rush.

They didn't know how far they had to ride and it didn't matter. Once saddled, they set a fast trail out of the stable again heading west. Their horses were well fed and rested and the two pushed them looking for that road the turned left. The morning sun was at their backs and the air was cool. As they rode the high ground side by side, they could see below in the distance the road that beckoned them.

As one they reined in. When they got to the left turn, they reined to a stop to give Crown's horses a breather. "You know Pat, these are pretty fair horses." Pat reached down and patted his mount on the neck. "Yeah, he has an eye for horse flesh," Pat answered.

The deep ruts in the road were running parallel to the pine covered mountain some ten miles to their left. Between them and the mountain, it quickly dropped down to flatter level ground. After cooling their horses an hour or so, they picked up the pace but not enough to tire the mounts.

Just as they had been told by the sheriff, the ground turned white, dry, and barren. Now both men could feel the hot sun beating down on their backs. The horses kicked up white dust coating their hooves as they walked. "Able said this wouldn't last long," Jake commented. Jake reached down and untied his canteen then took a big drink. Pat lifted his to check the fill. "I filled them both this morning," Jake said.

They had been in what one could only describe as a desert about two hours when the green started to reappear. As they rode, they noticed the road angled slightly towards the ridge, closing the distance between them and the mountain where they knew Crown to be.

It was Jake who first saw the white

sheep peacefully grazing next to the red and white cattle. Now the mid-day sun pounded down on them, only the cool breeze kept the sweat from running down their faces. Pat, always on the hunt, spotted a dark green line running across the pasture perpendicular to the road. He knew soon they would ride up on a creek or ditch and there they would water their horses.

It wasn't long when they rode up to the edge of a nicely size little creek. They walked their mounts to center stream and reined in, then Jake climbed out of the saddle and stood in the cool mountain water that went halfway to his boot tops. While his horse drank, he untied his bandana and swished it through the water, then retied it back loosely, around his neck.

Pat had stretched out the looking glass and scanned back and forth across the pasture looking for any sign of movement. Then suddenly, he stood in the stirrups and stared off into the distance. Jake looked up at him and knew something caught his attention.

What Pat had seen as he searched the open field was a single rider and what he thought to be a pack horse moving at a trot beyond where he thought the house might be. "Look at this Jake," Pat said as he handed him the glass.

The distance was so great one couldn't make out anything except the two horses and a slight bit of dust trailing from behind the pack horse that was heading in the direction they now rode.

Jake saw the horses and handed the glass back to Pat. "You figure that's him?" Jake asked. "That's either him or someone taking him grub," Pat said, then he put the glass back to his eye. With the glass he back- trailed the rider in the direction he had to come from. "The house is up here a short piece, I'd bet on it " he said as he stared. "That rider came from there and we'll arrive shortly," Pat said.

Jake climbed back into the saddle and slowly nudged the horse out of the cool water. Pat relaxed the glass and dropped it back into his bags before he touched his spurs to the horse and moved to Jake's side.

Back into the ruts they rode. As they rode around a sharp turn, they saw the ranch house less than a half-mile off. Before they got to the house, they passed under a wooden sign that said, Razor livestock Company. This sign was much like the one at the Rising Sun.

Approaching the house Jake unlashed his Colt and loosened it in his holster. Pat took his badge out of his pocket and pinned it to his shirt. They knew they were being watched, strangers riding up to a secluded house such as this were always seen and more than likely under someone's rifle.

Sometimes, but not always, the sight of a badge would make things easier. Fifty yards shy of the main house the door swung open. This ranch house was like most ranch houses. White-washed walls under a cedar shake roof like this were common in Colorado. Barns, corrals, grain silos and windmills were all a part of ranching and farming. These things were a necessities that a rancher or farmer had to have to survive in the west.

A half dozen chickens pecked and scratched at the mud and manure around the water trough. A black dog got to his feet and stood stiff- legged and barked as they rode up. As they rode in, Jake noticed four saddle horses in the big corral next to the barn. When the door swung open, a shotgun toting woman wearing a red plaid apron stepped out of the house and into the shade of the porch. When she saw the badge, she seemed to relax and lowered the scattergun, seeing this Jake and Pat reined in about ten yards from the porch.

Jake turned and looked to his right to see she was backed up by two men, one of which looked to be a boy in his mid-teens standing in front of big barn. They didn't have scatter guns, they had Winchester rifles. A young girl that looked to be around twelve stood to the side of her mother in the shade of the porch.

As a sign of respect, both men took

off their hats. "Good afternoon maam. I'm Pat Brennon, U. S. Marshall. Is your husband home? I'd like to have a word with him," he said? "It's OK Gordon, he's a U.S. Marshall," she said. Just then, the two men with rifles approached from their right. Jake saw them glance over at the Crown brands on the horses they rode.

The older of the two was wearing bib-overalls with a big floppy brimmed hat and anyone could see he had a mouth full of tobacco. The younger of the two was hatless and walked a little behind, it was obvious he two had a mouth full of tobacco., Jake could see a brown tobacco stain on his chin.

"You care to climb down Marshall?" he asked. Slowly, they climbed out of the saddle. When Jake had both feet on the ground, he tried to stretch the kinks out of his back. "I'm Gordon Cutter and this is my wife, Silvia. Cleat he's my son and that's' my girl Carol. We own the Razor," he proudly said. "Come up here on the porch out of the sun, Marshall," he added.

Hat in hand, Jake and Pat walked up on the porch. " You and your friend take a load off Marshall," Gordon said, as he pointed to two chairs. "Gordon, he's Jake Cleary," Pat said. Jake nodded as to say hi. "Well Gordon, we need to know if anyone rode by here in the last day or two?" Pat asked. "No Marshall. I ain't seen a soul," he answered. Hearing that response he knew was a lie, affirmed to Jake that it was Crown ahead of that pack horse. Jake noticed the woman look away as her husband spoke. He could tell she wasn't comfortable hearing her husband lie to a Marshall.

Pat also knew he was lying but couldn't say anything to embarrass him in front of his wife. "Well Gordon, I know you have kin named Forest Crown and that's who we're looking for. I was in hopes you could help us find him."

"Marshall, Forest Crown is my cousin on my mother's side. I haven't seen forest in years," Gordon replied. The two got to their feet and stepped off the porch, Jake put his hat on as did Pat. "We know he's in those mountains: we tracked him for a while, so we thought we could head him off this way," Pat said as he climbed into the saddle. Jake was anxious to leave, he knew they were close to Crown and he didn't want to lose any more time.

Jake respectfully touched the brim of his hat to acknowledge the lady, then spurred his horse north. Gordon stepped off the porch and watched them ride out of sight past the house and beyond the barn. He looked down and shook his head. "You did your best Gordon; he may be kin but don't let him get you killed. Couldn't you tell those two men are going to kill him? You keep out of this," Silvia said as the screen door closed.

They both figured the man they'd seen had to be Crown; but they couldn't be sure until they looked him in the face. There were still several hours of daylight left and they wanted to use every minute of it. knowing they were just a couple hours behind the man they hunted.

To the west, they slightly turned

knowing they would cut the pack horse's trail. At a fast trot, they moved until Jake overrode the trail they hunted. Turning back around, he came to a quick stop in the middle of the dirt trail and Pat was soon at his side.

"We're less than two hours behind him Pat. I'm gonna push him, I want you to keep an eye on our back trail, after all, they are kin,"Jake said. Pat knew exactly what Jake was referring to and he was right: kin don't usually go against family and that was a concern.

Jake moved out, once again set his spurs and the mare lunged forward and ran the trail like she knew what her rider wanted. Pat waited a couple minutes, then moved to a fast trot and watched Jake's dust until he could no longer see his friend, occasionally stopping to check their back trail as Jake had asked.

Jake had been pushing nearly an hour when he reined in at a small narrow creek. His horse was breathing hard and so was he. This is where he would let his mount water and cool down for a short time, giving Pat time to close the distance between them.

With reins in hand, Jake climbed out of the saddle and dropped to his knees and splashed the cool water in his face. He studied the tracks of the two horses and saw Crown had watered here too. The trail had been slowly rising into the foothills, putting him in a position where he could look down on the valley he had just rode through. He looked down into the valley at the tall grass and the streams that seemed to keep everything green. He saw a half dozen deer peacefully feeding on the tall grass. *This is some great land for raising cattle,* he thought.

It was midafternoon when a heavy breeze came out of the south pushing dark, gray, low hanging clouds in his direction. Jake remounted and looked at his back trail seeing Pat a half mile back coming at a steady trot. *That's all we need now, heavy rain,* Jake thought. Moving at a slow walk, he watched the trail. A hundred yards beyond the creek the tracks turned left taking him directly toward the mountain.

After the abrupt left turn, the trail now got steeper and the flat ground was replaced with small, rolling hills all the way to the base of the mountain. The trail now ran up and down and over the small hills and dips. The foothills turned to bare ground sprinkled with sage and an occasional scrub oak, but mostly white dirt and small surface rocks covered everything. As they walked, Jake could hear the click of hoofs on the rocks. Crown had no idea he was being followed, so he made no attempt to hide or cover his tracks.

Jake was about to follow the trail up and over a small rise when some instinct told him to rein-in. He had learned over the years in the army to trust his instincts, so he pulled his horse to a stop and he slowly dismounted.

Cautiously, he tied off to a scrub oak then loosened his Colt in his holster and pulled his rifle out of the scabbard. Slowly, he started the short walk up the hill. Just as his eyes were level with the top of the hill, he saw the glare off a windowpane.

Quickly, he dropped down into a squatting position then looked back for Pat. Not seeing him, he took off his hat and laid down on his belly and slowly crawled a few feet up to where he could see over the crest of the hill.

Six to seven-hundred yards from where he lay, he could plainly see the front of a small line shack. He had seen and spent many nights in shacks such as these, listening to the wind whistling between the wood planks and he could tell by the large corral and the tin roof this was a line shack like many he'd slept in.

These shacks were built miles from the main bunk house, giving the cowboys a place to sleep out of the weather while they were protecting the interest of the ranch. Every shack Jake had seen had one room, usually with two cots and a wood stove sitting in the middle of the floor and a small table with a couple chairs. These shacks were built as close to water as possible, eliminating the chore of hauling water not only for themselves, but for the horses they rode.

Jake could see from where he laid the two horses, they followed were drinking from a small grass lined stream that trickled through the corral. He rolled over and looked back to see Pat climbing out of the saddle. Just then, a sliver of blue light slipped through the dark clouds on the far side of the valley and was quickly followed by the roar of thunder, causing the horses to spook slightly.

Jake put on his hat and walked back down the hill to where Pat stood. "Whoever had the pack horse in tow is in a shack up there a piece," Jake said. Just then, the thunder roared again and the horses again flinched. "What you got in mind Jake?" Pat asked. Jake looked into the dark sky as the clouds moved even closer.

"I got no intention of sleeping in this rain while that old coot sleeps under a dry roof," Jake answered. Pat grinned a little. " You remember Levi telling us only a rifle and a scattergun was gone out of that rack. Well Pat, we got the rifle. I figure on riding over that hill and I'm betting all he has is the shotgun.," Jake said. Pat stood silent, slapping the palm of his gloved hand with his reins as he frequently did, then he climbed into the saddle.

"Mount up. I ain't waiting 'til dark," Pat said. Jake nodded in agreement and climbed into the saddle.

CHAPTER

15

Once in the saddle, Jake pulled his Colt and spun the cylinder. Pat pulled his Winchester and fed three more rounds into the tube then looked at Jake and gave him a nod, before they both clicked their horses forward.

Neither men had seen Forest Crown in over two years. All they knew about him was that he was totally ruthless and had hired and paid at least a half-dozen gunmen to kill them by any means necessary.

Now they had reason to believe he was holed up in the line shack just over the small hill. The one thing they knew for sure was he was armed with a double barreled, twelve gauge, Coach gun, which at close range was totally devastating if you were on the wrong end of those barrels.

They had been on his trail for weeks now, the way they figured it, it had to come to an end today one way or another. They were tired of hunting and being hunted, they were fed up with sleeping with their fingers wrapped around a gun. They'd had enough trail grub and the hunt for Forest Crown was coming to a quick end.

As they rode over the crest of the slight hill, the shack came into full view for the first time. The small building sat facing west, the setting sun glaring off the dirty window. A little stream running through the corral filling a small, shallow basin a dozen yards across before it ran out the opposite side.

When they came into view, a coyote, standing on the edge of the little tarn, looked up from the water and silently trotted off. A white, long-legged stork of some kind looked at them with no concern and kept wading in the shallow water.

On the far end of the corral, away from the shack, the two horses stood against the fence in the shade of an old aspen tree. The two men sat in silence, looking for any movement in the little building. The only sound was that of two crows squawking somewhere in the distance. The fresh, clean smell of rain filled the air.

All of a sudden, a streak of blue light slithered through the sky quickly followed by the roar of close thunder. This time, the loud snap of the lightning and the roar of the thunder surprised both men and horses, causing both horses to bolt forward and whinny. Both Jake and Pat had to lock their knees and grab the reins with both hands to pull the startled animals back into control.

Once the horses were settled down, they nudged them forward and moved even closer to the shack. Again, they reined in. Pat held his Winchester across his lap and they watched. With a slight touch, Jake moved his horse to within thirty yards of the shack.

Without warning, the front door flew open. Taking long, angry steps, Forest Crown, still in a white shirt and cravat with a black leather strap running across his chest, stepped onto the narrow porch. The sawed-off double barrel he held firmly in both hands was pointed directly at the two.

"You two have haunted me long enough," he hollered. Before they could react, the shotgun barked and belched white and orange smoke out of both barrels at the same time.

From where they sat, the thirty yards was a little past the effective range for a shotgun with barrels of this length.

By the time Jake and Pat saw the fire and smoke they felt the pellets. both horses leapt into the air twisting and letting out frantic criesas the best of the pellets hit both horses directly in the face, quickly throwing Jake and Pat to the ground.

As they hit the ground, Jake ripped his Colt from his holster and fired one quick shot. At the same time, Pat still on his knees with his rifle in one hand dropped the hammer as he tried to get to his feet. In the split of a second, Crown was slammed back against the wall as the empty shotgun tumbled to the ground. Without a thought, Jake re cocked and fired once more. As Pat regained his footing, he cocked the rifle and planted another slug deep in Crown's chest.

Forest Crown piled up and rolled off the porch where he lay face down in the dirt on a late afternoon, the victim of his own hateful revenge.

Jake and Pat, both stunned, clumsily got to their feet and stood for a short second to catch their breath.

Jake had small trickles of blood running down his face and off his ear. Pat had little streaks of blood running from his hairline and the bridge of his nose and off his chin. On both men little spots of crimson started appearing on the front of their shirts from the few pellets that made their way past the horses.

Seeing Crown was dead, Jake turned and quickly glanced up at their horses. Down the slope in the shallow water hole both horses wandered and stumbled, aimlessly shaking their heads from side to side. Their faces too were covered with blood from their ears to their nostrils. Pat slowly walked up to the porch and dropped down hard. Jake came up and dropped down at his side.

"How bad you hit Pat?" Jake asked. Pat turned slightly and looked at Jake. "About the same as you," he answered. Then their attentions turned to the wounded horses. "I wonder how bad they are," Jake said. "We came out of it a hell of a lot better than they did I'm betting," Pat answered.

They sat for a couple minutes watching the confused horses stumble around, both knowing Crown's horses were done. Slowly, they stood on unsteady legs, Pat took his bandana from around his neck and softly wiped the blood out of his eyes. Jake reached up and felt his right ear to make sure it was still there. Pat looked over at him and commented, "Don't worry, only one bb went clean through.

When they tried to approach the injured horses, the horses hearing their boots on the ground snorted slightly and backed away closer to the edge of the water. Slowly, Jake and Pat approached only to have the frightened horses move into the pool. Once Jake and Pat stepped into the water the wounded horses near panic could no longer hear their footsteps.

"Woah, easy now girl," Jake said in a calm tone to reassure the frightened horses. Gently, he moved up to the mare he rode and laid his hand on her rump as he kept repeating the words "easy, easy girl." Once he could reach the reins, he picked them up out of the water and walked around to see how bad she was wound.

What he saw sickened him, even more now

he wanted Crown dead. The wounds he saw were much worse than he imagined. The frightened horse could no longer see the man that spoke so gently to her. Softly, he spoke to her as he led her away from the shallow water where she stood in total fear and darkness.

Once away, he looked at Pat, who was in the brown water up to his knees leading the bleeding horse out of the pond. Gently, Pat took his bloody bandana and rinsed it in the water and slowly wiped what blood he could off the frightened horses face. Jake could tell when Pat looked away, the horse he led was in just as bad a shape as his own.

Slowly and gently, they led the horses to dry ground and brought them together all the time speaking softly to calm them. When Pat reached Jake, he took Jake's reins and one at a time Jake dropped their saddles and set them aside. "Jake, reach in my saddle bags," Pat said. He didn't have to be told, he saw Pat's pistol wasn't on his side. When Jake handed Pat his Colt, Pat turned slightly and covered the gun with his hand to muffle the sound of the gun being cocked. Jake slowly, drew his pistol and they made sure the two shots sounded as one.

It was over in a second, the one responsibility all horsemen hate more than anything. Silence hovered over the two men like the gray clouds that followed them this day. Without a word, they picked up their saddles and walked back to the line shack that would protect them from the rain that had started to fall.

When they stepped up on the porch, Jake kicked the coach gun aside and stripped Crown of his shoulder rig before walking inside. Pat stopped and looked down at forest Crown, who was now being drenched with the cold rain. "You lived too long old man, we should have killed you two years ago," Pat mumbled and walked through the door.

They didn't know when, nor did they care, but sometime during the night the rain had quit pounding on the tin roof. Crown had brought a pack horse loaded with enough food to last a man for several weeks. With the rise of the sun, Jake sat up on the edge of his cot and looked around, then started throwing kindling in the small stove.

"I know that pack horse belongs to the Razor and I want Gordon to watch me ride through the ranch with his horse under me. So, let's get some breakfast down, I wanna take this ride," Jake said as he unbuttoned his shirt.   By now the bb's that were too deep to pick out had scabbed over and Jake wiped them with his whiskey-soaked bandana. Pat, with the same problem, had bumps from bb's on his chin and forehead. "You know if they got a doc. in Rocky Ford?" Jake asked. "Well, if they don't, I know they got one in La 'Junta, Pat answered.

While Jake was buttoning his shirt, Pat dumped Crown's bags on the table and found a leather pouch with more gold coins. "You wanna leave these eagles here for Gordon?" he said sardonically. "The way I figure it Pat, Crown owes me them eagles for taking care of those horses he shot."

It wasn't long and the two set a trail for the Razor. The horse Pat rode had the Crown brand, but Jake rode in on the mount with the Razor brand burnt on his hip.

When they rode back into the ranch, Gordon, with a cheek full of tobacco, stood with his son Clete, next to the house and watched Jake ride in on his brand. Pat reined in long enough for Gordon to see their bb holes and the blood on their shirts. Then Pat spoke with a voice filled with anger. " Forest and all that grub is up at your line shack. When you go, you might wanna take some shovels because you have dead horses at you're front porch. You can dump Mr. Crown in with the horses, that'll save you digging one more hole. Oh and you can pick up your horse in La 'Junta." Then just as quick as he stopped, he reined about and rode out of sight. Gordon and the boy never spoke.

It was late afternoon when they rode into Rocky Ford and they tied up at the sheriff's office. Just as their boots hit the ground, Able walked up and looked at them a second. "The doc's office is across the street and down a ways I can see both of ya need to see him," he said.

Tired and sore, they walked across the street and into the office they'd been looking for. Before they left the old doctor's office, he dropped seventeen number six bbs in a white porcelain pan and demanded three dollars which they happily paid.

When they walked into the hotel, they asked the old clerk. "Are our two rooms still empty?" They didn't bother to eat, they were too sore to do anything but try to sleep it off.

In the early morning they sent telegrams to Durango, then rode back to the Crown ranch and reclaimed their own horses. Jake was anxious to get to the Rising Sun and back on his three-year-old. It was long after dark and the ride from Rocky Ford to La' Junta was silent. From there, silence followed them through town and back home. They were tired and sore and wanted to sleep in their own beds. Pat never said a word when he turned off, towards Two Rivers and Jake finished the ride home on a horse he hadn't named yet.

Made in the USA
Monee, IL
24 June 2021